PENGUIN MET

REMEMBER ME AS YOURS

Novoneel Chakraborty is the prolific author of eighteen bestselling thriller novels, two e-novellas and one bestselling short-story collection. His works have been translated into multiple Indian languages. Almost all his novels have debuted on top three Nielsen listings across India.

His Forever series made it to *Times of India*'s Most Stunning Books of 2017 list, while the Stranger trilogy became a phenomenal hit among young adults, with Amazon tagging it, along with his erotic thriller *Black Suits You*, as their memorable reads of the year. Selling over one million copies, he is India's most popular thriller novelist. His solid plotting, unpredictable twists and strong female protagonists have earned him the moniker 'Sidney Sheldon of India'.

The Stranger trilogy, his immensely popular thriller series, has been translated into six Indian languages. The trilogy has also been adapted into a successful web series by Applause Entertainment and Rose Audio Visuals on MX Player, amassing a whopping 500-million plus views. Other successful adaptations for the screen include *Black Suits You* and the Forever series.

Novoneel has written several hit TV and original web shows for premier channels like MX Player, Sony, Star Plus, Zee and Zee5. He lives and works in Mumbai.

ALSO BY THE AUTHOR

Half Torn Hearts

The Best Couple Ever

Cheaters

FOREVER SERIES

Forever Is A Lie

Forever Is True

THE STRANGER TRILOGY

Marry Me Stranger

All Yours Stranger

Forget Me Not Stranger

EX

How About a Sin Tonight?

Black Suits You

Roses Are Blood Red

Cross Your Heart, Take My Name

Whisper to Me Your Lies

A Thousand Kisses Deep

Heart on the Edge

Remember Me as Yours

They went to look for love.
They found life.

NOVONEEL CHAKRABORTY

An imprint of Penguin Random House

PENGUIN METRO READS

Penguin Metro Reads is an imprint of the Penguin Random House group of companies whose addresses can be found at global.penguinrandomhouse.com

Published by Penguin Random House India Pvt. Ltd
4th Floor, Capital Tower 1, MG Road,
Gurugram 122 002, Haryana, India

First published in Penguin Metro Reads by Penguin Random House India 2024

10 9 8 7 6 5 4 3 2 1

ISBN 9780143467526

Typeset in Requiem Text by Manipal Technologies Limited, Manipal
Printed at Replika Press Pvt. Ltd, India

www.penguin.co.in

To that thing which belongs to us
but we can't keep for ourselves: innocence.

GIRL ONE

1

It was the last day of Navratri. Nityami, who took her social and religious duties very seriously, had done her puja in the morning, pleading to the Goddess for a continuous three minutes to forgive her for accepting the sinful offer from her boyfriend the other day—one which her mind wasn't letting her accept while her hormones weren't letting her refuse. At her age, the hormones rightfully won.

It was a Sunday. After going through the usual round of inconsequential chit-chat with her parents, after her puja, Nityami messaged her boyfriend, Raghav, and went to her room to busy herself with a shopping app. That was one relationship which always went smoothly. Half of her salary went into buying clothes, footwear, perfume and cosmetics. Though she didn't have many places to go or people to meet, the act of carefully stocking them in her wardrobe itself was a thrill. Her everyday routine was about travelling from home to office to home until Raghav stepped into her life recently, which stretched her loop to office–meeting Raghav–home. But that was more of a weekend loop. She was supposed to meet him today to discuss the sinful offer, but because of a get-together with her college friends in the evening, she had to postpone it.

Nityami was meeting her college girl gang, together, after seven years. They were six of them, of whom five had left Bhopal right after college for work. Only Nityami was left behind, choosing to work in Bhopal. Sitting in her Uber in a white Zara top and a long skirt, she was reminiscing about the last day in college when all of them were emotional, had scribbled on each other's dresses and promised to keep the bond alive throughout their lives. Nityami didn't know which one was worse. That over time, things faded away. Or, that not a single one of them complained about this fact. Not even in their WhatsApp group. Text messages, funny forwards and sometimes some gossip was what kept them in touch. Nobody knew what was happening with the other at a personal level. Nobody had time. It was as if people had accepted the fading away as something that normally happened to people, to friendships. Not Nityami. She missed those times. More so because she could never make the kind of friends she did when she was in college. She had become a loner ever since.

As the thoughts of days gone by hovered over her, Nityami opened Instagram on her phone. She checked the stories of her friends one by one and realized each of the other five had uploaded a story of them being excited to meet their girl gang. One clicked herself at a spa; another from a boutique while choosing her outfit for the occasion; a third was in a beauty parlour having a hair spa done; the fourth was at a nail studio while the fifth girl had posted her picture from a five-star hotel where she was having breakfast. The caption read: *not having much coz need to have a lot of goss in the evening when I meet my cuties.* Along with the others, the location was also tagged. Nityami re-shared the tagged stories on her Instagram story. Then social-media anxiety pushed her to think that she too should post one such 'cool' story and tag her friends. But what should it be? She quickly changed the destination in her Uber app to the nearest Starbucks.

Nityami reached the Starbucks in the next five minutes. Ordered a regular-sized Americano, as a takeaway, put her phone on a timer and clicked herself with the coffee and a caption: 'Sipping caffeine, for tonight's going to be a long, long night!' Nityami posted it, tagging her friends and feeling proud of her prompt thinking. She booked another Uber to actually go to the mall where she was supposed to meet her friends. Suddenly, the cab bumped over a speed breaker. Nityami, who was sipping her coffee at the time, squeezed the mug hard, which made the already loosely attached cap come out. The coffee spilt over her white top. For that fraction of a second, Nityami wanted to convince herself it was one of the innumerable nightmares she had seen in life. But it wasn't. A stain had already formed on her top. By the time the cab reached the mall, Nityami knew what she had to do. Rush to a clothing store.

She had reached the mall around half an hour before the get-together. Of which twenty-five minutes had gone by. She couldn't find anything nice to wear. And the tops she liked were not in her size. The analogy of all this to her life was so painstakingly close that only Nityami knew she was on the verge of crying. Her phone buzzed. It was Nidhi.

'Where are you? We all are here.' She said in an excited tone.

'Reaching in two minutes,' Nityami said, laying her hand on a blue top. Her size wasn't available so she chose a larger one. She quickly paid for it, went to the washroom and then changed to the new top. She thrust the coffee-stained white one into her bag and rushed outside to the restaurant where they were supposed to meet.

The initial two minutes of seeing and meeting the old pals were indeed exciting. And then it occurred to Nityami that all of them had changed. Although she still carried mental images of her friends as they had been seven years ago, today it seemed she was interacting with five strangers, who seemed to connect with each other smoothly, but Nityami was finding it difficult to bond with them. She preferred to keep quiet and listen to them. They were full of their experiences of the big cities, workplaces, men and travel. There was both a sense of confidence in them as there was a degree of pretence. Nityami could sense it. It was as though much of what they were saying was simply for effect. As if they all had something to sell to the others.

Nidhi was selling her great sex life with her man.

Prachi was selling how a big city had triggered the bohemian side in her.

Nilanjana was selling how she had learnt to be detached from her family in Bhopal.

Swati was selling how it was sexy for single girls to date married men since they won't ever step into your private space and be clingy.

While Megha was selling how important it is to get married early and have kids too. She was pregnant with her first kid.

Nityami felt that somewhere, they all knew they weren't living the lives they thought they would be. And so, their need to push what they were living as something to be aspired for was coming out a little too desperately.

'Why are you so quiet? What's happening in your life, girl?' Nidhi asked.

For a moment, Nityami's mind went blank. What's happening in my life, really? Then she looked at the five faces gawking at her for a response.

Great sex. Great job. And great boyfriend.' Nityami said and immediately realized she perhaps hadn't got the chronology right. To salvage herself, she quickly added, 'Whom I'm going to marry very soon.'

'Congrats,' Nidhi said. Others followed and then nobody asked her anything else. The four hours that Nityami sat there, she spoke the least and heard the most. They ordered their starters, drinks, main course and lastly, dessert. In between, Nidhi and Prachi excused themselves to smoke. Nilanjana used that time to scroll through her phone while Swati excused herself to talk to her sugar daddy. Megha got busy video-calling her kid and forcing Nityami to be a part of it. The latter excused herself for the washroom.

She felt relieved standing alone in the washroom. Her phone flashed Raghav's name. She picked up the call.

'So, the evening has stretched into dinner.'

'Yeah, you know how it is when you meet old friends,' Nityami said. She didn't want to come across as someone with weird friends to her current boyfriend.

'I do. Moreover, you chose them over me so it better be good company.'

Nityami sensed some spite in his voice.

'Are you angry?' she asked.

'No. Pissed off, but it's okay. I'm fine now. We are meeting tomorrow anyway, right?' he said, referring to the sinful proposal he had given her.

Nityami paused for a few seconds before saying a meek 'yes'. Raghav took it as shyness.

'I like that,' he said. Nityami started getting a call from Nidhi.

'My friends are calling me.'

'All right, call me when you reach home.'

'Sure,' Nityami said and joined her friends outside only to learn they had called for the cheque. That, for Nityami, was the best thing about the get-together.

While going back home in an Uber, Nityami passed by the hotel where she was supposed to check in the next morning. Raghav would be waiting for her, as per his sinful proposal, and she was supposed to gift him her virginity.

2

Nityami Thakur looked in the mirror and cursed herself for choosing Neha's parlour over Beauty Plus parlour. She always used to go to the latter but she had run out of things on which she could blame her relationship misfortunes. Her last date—the tenth in a year before she met Raghav—had gone wrong, and she thought the one thing that was bringing her bad luck was the parlour. Maybe something was wrong with their facial. With their hair spa. With the whole goddamn beauty parlour itself. Before the smart part of her brain could tell her all this was bullshit, she shut it up. She was already done blaming everyone and everything else. Hence, this time it was Neha's parlour.

What irked her was the obvious difference between her two eyebrows. It was a threading gone wrong. And she couldn't cancel the date. She had already done it twice a week ago. But that was just a coffee meet. And she cancelled it because she was feeling bloated. The week that followed was all about work pressure. Then the girl-gang thing happened. Finally, the subsequent weekend came and it was time for the different kind of date Raghav had proposed.

'Let's meet at an OYO room,' he had said over the phone. Nityami swallowed a lump in her throat. She knew what the connotation of an OYO room was. Though she was actually a virgin, she had told Raghav a lie that she had a boyfriend with whom she had been intimate. Nityami realized by now that it was all right to tell a guy about one boyfriend, or else she would run the risk of being interpreted as boring. More than one, and the boy would run the risk of feeling threatened and also judge her character. Thus, she had told Raghav only about one imaginary boyfriend. The truth was, she never had a boyfriend. From the time she felt her hormones handholding her into puberty, she had a crush on one boy in school. The crush eventually turned into such an intense fixation that Nityami thought she would just remain in love with him, and he would never know it. The power of unreciprocated love. It can numb the sensible part of your brain for quite some time. For Nityami, it remained so until she turned twenty-three.

Looking around, she realized she too deserved a boyfriend. She knew someone must have been made for her; it was just that she didn't think seeking him out would be such heartachingly hard work that even by twenty-seven, she wouldn't be successful in finding THE man for her. There were plenty of options for the trending NATO (Not-Attached-To-Outcome) dating amongst youngsters, but Nityami wasn't exactly looking for that. That was till she met Raghav via Bumble a month ago. Their connection seemed to run at top gear. They met, they conversed, they liked each other; he told his parents first, then she told her parents and now, a month after their first date at a café, the families had locked a date for the engagement in the coming week and the wedding seven months later. It all happened so fast that Nityami didn't know how to react. Perhaps that's how life operates, she told herself. A long dry spell and then so much rain that you didn't know whether to enjoy it or run for cover.

Standing in front of her bedroom mirror, Nityami knew she didn't want to screw this up. If Raghav had called her to an OYO room, she knew he probably wanted to check their sexual compatibility. And rightly so. Though she wasn't experienced enough to even understand what sexual compatibility was, going by what she heard from her experienced friends, all she knew was if the guy could go for more than half an hour, then it was a green light. One final look at her eyebrows and she convinced herself that nothing could be done now. Instead of him discovering it, Nityami thought, she would point out the faux pas herself when she met him in an hour. He probably wouldn't mind it so much then.

Nityami was dressed casually but that was going to change. She always used to dress casually to go out of her house because she didn't want her parents to know she was going out on a date. On date-days, she used to reach a nearby mall well before time, change, put on some make-up and then visit the café or restaurant to meet her date. And before coming back home, she would pretend in front of the guy that she was waiting for her Uber. When he left, she would invariably go back to the mall, change and finally head home. It would spare her all the unnecessary questions her parents would have asked otherwise. Even though they were involved in Raghav's case, she still couldn't tell her parents she was going to an OYO room with him.

Nityami left the house saying she was going to meet a college friend. That too triggered a set of questions from her mother:

Which college friend?

What is she doing now?

Is she married?

Kids?

How is her marriage going?

Is she settled here or abroad?

Nityami knew if the answers were negative, her mother would still be filled with a weird positivity. She would be convinced that her daughter wasn't the only one suffering in the world. This time, before her mother could even ask who the friend was, Nityami left, saying her Uber had arrived.

It took her fifteen minutes to reach the nearest mall. She went to the washroom, took out her outfit—a red top and a black palazzo she'd ordered online—and in ten minutes when she exited the washroom, she looked more confident than ever.

During her Uber auto ride from the mall to the OYO hotel, Nityami suddenly started feeling nervous. She had never been naked in front of a man. And she didn't have the perfect figure. She was slightly plump but thankfully, she had a good basal metabolic rate (BMR) so the fat was well distributed. She could feel gooseflesh thinking about what would happen in the room from the time she would enter it. Until that time, she had found Raghav very comfortable to be around. He never asked any awkward questions like the other guys she'd dated, nor did he have a condescending sense of humour where he belittled her and her attempts to be a working professional. Raghav didn't have any problem with her working after marriage. Thinking about Raghav, she started fantasizing about what they would do. Would they simply begin smooching, strip each other and talk only after they were done? Like she had seen in so many Hollywood films? Or would they converse a little, have some food and drink . . . Nityami remembered she had lied to him that she had never drunk alcohol. She did drink socially but the pressure of a 'correct' girl was something she started feeling when she entered the dating scene with marriage in mind. Casual dating didn't have those pressures, but the guys who were in the dating scene for marriage wanted a 'correct' girl. And a correct girl meant she shouldn't have any bad habits. Bad habits as defined by men, of course.

Nityami reached the OYO hotel.

'Are you inside?' she WhatsApped him on entering the lobby. Raghav was supposed to message her after he reached. He hadn't.

'Yes,' the response came. It was a three-star hotel. Nothing fancy. Nityami walked up to the reception, gave them her Aadhaar card, which they photocopied and gave the original back to her. Nityami looked around for the elevator. She took it and stepped out on to the first floor. Next, she looked for room number 106. As she stood in front of the door, she took a deep breath. Something unprecedented would have happened by the time she came out of the room.

She would lose her virginity and become someone's forever, she thought. She knocked on the door. A few seconds later, Raghav opened it. She was all smiles. He was all serious.

'What happened?' she asked, sensing something was gravely wrong. Raghav gave her an I-am-disappointed look and said, 'I can't believe you came here. You shouldn't have.'

'What, why?' *Did he already know the eyebrow disaster? That can be corrected; hope he knows that.*

Raghav, who was in formal wear, called out looking inside the room:

'Mom, Dad.'

His parents are here? Before Nityami could think any further, her would-be in-laws stood in front of her. And the look the three had on their faces made her feel really cheap.

'Will you please tell me what's happening here?' Nityami was already on the defensive. Raghav's response made her want to pinch herself so she could wake up and realize it was all a dream.

Unfortunately, it wasn't.

3

'This was a character test for you,' Raghav's father said.

'We wanted to see if you would say yes or no,' added Raghav's mother.

'I really thought you wouldn't come and we would go ahead with the relationship,' Raghav spoke up.

With the three standing right opposite her, giving her disgusted looks, Nityami was intimidated.

'I'm sorry. What should I do now?' she asked meekly.

'What do we know?' said Raghav's mother, the most aggressive of the trio. 'I'll inform your parents we aren't interested in a girl who comes to OYO rooms.'

'But I came here to meet your son only.'

'Shut up!'

The mother pushed her aside and marched out of the room. So did the father. And finally Raghav.

'Please delete my number,' he said. Nityami stood there feeling like a fool as the three stepped into the elevator. Gingerly, she entered the room and closed the door behind her. She went to the bed like a zombie and sat on it. During moments like this, when she couldn't think of anything, feel anything or say anything, there was only one thing that came to her rescue. She picked up the landline phone and ordered a pizza and a Coke from room service. Then she burst into tears. What the fuck just happened? she wondered. Never for a moment since the time she first met Raghav did she expect him to pull off something like this. It was not just an insult to Nityami, but Raghav had shown her with his actions that she was a fool and had completely misread him. If not immediately, then in a few days' time, she would know how much her confidence would be punctured and then what? The same thing that happened after every guy left her: she would hate herself a little bit more.

The pizza and Coke arrived. Nityami watched *Tom and Jerry*, her favourite cartoon, on her phone while hogging the pizza. Then she slept like a child till the evening. She woke up to find seven missed calls from her mother. She checked out of the hotel, paid for the room and took an Uber auto home.

Two minutes before she reached her place, she got a message from her father.

Beta, come to the park first. I will see you there.

Okay papa, she messaged back and asked the Uber driver to stop in front of the park's main gate. It was a family park used by the residents around as a kids' playing area while the joggers' track built inside attracted the elderly of the neighbourhood.

Nityami understood the news of her being at the OYO hotel must have reached her parents. And her mother must have lost it. Her father, Raghuveer Singh Thakur, was always the one who took time to understand her side of the story, be it when she was in school, college or even during her work life. Nityami felt blessed to have a father like that.

Entering the park, she noticed her father walking on the joggers' track. She waved to him. Seeing her, he came forward. They met by an empty bench. At that time, there was nobody else in the park.

'Sit,' Mr Thakur said. Nityami did as asked.

'I think I already know what must have happened,' Mr Thakur began.

Nityami promised herself that she wouldn't cry in front of her father for she knew her tears affected his blood pressure, but she couldn't help it. She soon controlled herself.

'I'm all right, papa.'

'No, you're not. And I can feel it. You think if you don't tell your father everything, he won't ever get it?'

Nityami remained quiet.

'I'll handle your mother about today. But I wanted to meet you before to discuss what's happening. I've seen you the saddest in this last year or two.'

Nityami was glad someone understood her problems. Or at least saw she had some. But should she come out clean to her father, knowing he was a hypertension patient? She knew he would keep thinking about her problems day and night and then it could result in him being hospitalized. Her papa was her hero once, and he still was, but now because of his age, she couldn't thrust all her problems on her hero. It would be selfish on her part, Nityami thought.

'I'm twenty-seven, papa. There are so many things: work, boyfriends, career ahead, so I remain a little preoccupied. But that's about it. Nothing more, you chill.'

Mr Thakur gave his daughter a long stare. She responded with a glance and a question.

'Achcha, tell me, papa, did you also have relationship issues when you guys were young?'

'We were more of an obedient generation. We did what we were told. But, to be honest, that was also because the social design was a little different back then.'

'How so?'

'For example, fewer people used to go to big cities compared to today, and as a result, most families remained a joint family. And till you don't live alone, all by yourself, you won't experiment much with life. Now, it's the need of the hour.'

'Experiment?'

'No, living by oneself. So many youngsters are living away from their families. Even the kids of business families are taking up blue-collar jobs and moving away. Thus, their approach to life, their daily living habits, etc., are also different from what they used to be. Just imagine if there were smartphones and dating apps back in our times; it would still be difficult to meet up without being noticed by a family member or an acquaintance. Now that's not the case for the ones living in a third city, where they only have friends, not family or relatives.'

'That's true. Even all my friends have gone away from Bhopal.'

Mr Thakur put an arm around his daughter and said warmly, 'I know you don't like it here much, even though you grew up here.'

'I love the place. It's my city. It's just that I feel sometimes I have outgrown the place. I mean, I feel my desires are more modern than the place's vibe.'

'I know what you mean. I used to feel the same when I was growing up in Vidisha. Then we shifted to Bhopal.'

Mr Thakur's phone started ringing. It was his wife.

He hung up and said, 'I'm going home. You come after five minutes. And you know the drill, right? Just hear out what your mother says. No response. I'll handle her.'

'Sure, papa.' She gave her father a tight hug and watched him walk out of the park. Sitting alone, under the night sky, Nityami imagined the face of a particular boy in front of her eyes. Where was he now? What must he be doing? Is he married? With kids? How lucky that girl would be. This boy was her school crush. Someone she had not been able to track after they left school nor was she able to forget. And in moments like this, when yet another guy brought her to the edge where she didn't know whether she'd be able, once again, to believe a guy or not, that boy used to be her hope. At least someone somewhere was exactly the way she envisioned a 'man'. The sad part was she didn't know where he was.

After listening to her mother for a good one hour, till she retired to her room for the night, Nityami finally lay down on her bed. She opened Instagram on her phone. As she started scrolling, she looked through her friends' profiles. Some were enjoying themselves in the Maldives, some were trying on new outfits in a trial room and asking their lakhs of followers to help them choose, some mom bloggers were going on relentlessly about what young mothers should do, some were solo-travelling to unheard-of locations while some were displaying their tight booties from the gym. What was she doing? With 113 followers and a maximum of forty likes per post and twenty views of her stories? Was she this insignificant? Most of her batchmates were not even working. They had their IIT-IIM husbands who were earning for them. But the one who was feeling depressed was Nityami. Even after working in the Indian National Bank (INB), taking care of her own needs and sponsoring her own small holidays, she was the one made to believe by the social media society that she was a loser. Nityami wanted to smash the phone on the wall. Raghav's face flashed before her. The first thing she did was unfollow him and block him as well. Is trusting someone a fault these days? Nityami asked herself. And if not trust, how else was a relationship supposed to progress? A strong sense of revenge engulfed her. She would screw one—at least one guy—very badly. Toy with his emotions and then leave him feeling bad about himself. The want became a need in a few seconds. But how would she do it?

Nityami created a new Gmail ID. Using that, she set up a new Instagram ID. She went on a rampage to follow 1500 men. Some of them followed her back as well, taking her follower count to 200. This was more than her OG account, only because she had a girl with her tongue out as her DP and her bio read: Bored of carnivores. Looking for *cunt*ivores.

Nityami pulled the top of her night suit down, clicked a picture of her full, juicy boobs barring the nipples and made it the first post of her fake account whose handle she named *Naagin_ki_naani.*

She knew she would get DMs from guys. After which she would select one and screw him up badly. Nityami kept her phone by her side and went to sleep holding a lot of grudges against the whole world.

She was in for a surprise in the morning.

4

Every time she went to sleep with a lot on her mind, she didn't hear the alarm. It was only when her father knocked on her door that Nityami woke up with a heavy head.

'Don't you have office today?' she heard her father ask.

'I do,' she said and stepped out of bed. Minutes later, she turned the knob of her rain shower in the attached washroom to feel the cold water cascade on her naked body. This was easily the best time of the day. Nobody to disturb her. Nityami was a Piscean, so the love for water was natural. But that was not the only reason why she loved the shower. It was her me-time where no interruptions ever happened. Feeling the water on herself, her mind started jogging. She never thought she would be single this soon again. Raghav had ticked all the boxes. She was sure they were getting married. Like dead sure. And then OYO happened. Was she seriously supposed to say no to Raghav when he proposed the OYO room scenario to her? How would she know what he had in mind? How does anyone know anything about the person with whom one is supposed to settle down?

Nityami's experience with men until then could be encapsulated in one word: confusing. Apart from the casual ones, in total, she had dated four men from the age of twenty-one to twenty-seven with whom something serious had happened. Or so she thought. Before that, she considered herself to be born only for a particular boy whom she could never tell that she was in love with him. Vedant Kaushal. But that was in school. At twenty-one, she met Aashiq Khan. It was not just his name but also his behaviour that was *filmi*. They had met at a café that she and her friend used to frequent. Aashiq used to play guitar there. And he played quite well. All romantic songs. Then he saw her and started dedicating all his songs to Nityami. It flattered her. No man before that had made her feel special. Aashiq did. The way he used to strum his guitar, singing the love songs and looking at her sharply, Nityami's heart started melting one day at a time. Till a time came when she started frequenting the café almost daily and without her friend. That emboldened Aashiq to talk to her.

'I don't know what your name is,' were his first words to her, 'but I want to call you Hoor.' Nityami knew what 'hoor' meant. A beauty. She blushed. And made Aashiq share the table with her that day. As they got talking, she learnt that he didn't work in the café, as she had thought, but the café was a place where he loved to showcase his talent.

'I'm an artist. A singer to be precise. And very soon my songs will rule the world.' Aashiq said. His eyes were dreamy and in them, Nityami saw a certain magic. They started meeting outside the café. The conversation mostly used to be about him, his dreams, his future, which Nityami didn't mind. In fact, he had a funny way of mouthing it all, which kept her engaged.

She never told her parents about Aashiq simply because of the religion factor. Nityami knew it would be a bone of contention but in her heart, she was also knitting a sweet future for both of them. Aashiq would become a rock star while she would do a government job so he didn't have to worry about the expenditure. It was a perfect combination, she knew.

Seven months of dating around the city, and the day finally came when Nityami went to the place where Aashiq lived. A typical bachelor pad where he stayed with two roommates. Neither were there when they came in. The two talked for some time and then it was time to get intimate, Nityami was particularly nervous. It was her first time. The kiss went smoothly, which gave her confidence. But once they undressed, what followed was something Nityami hadn't dreamt about in her wildest nightmares. Aashiq was unable to get it up. That was still all right for Nityami since she knew they were in love. And sometimes performance pressure could lead to such disasters.

'I know it's your first time. Mine too,' she said. Aashiq gave her a bewildered look and said, 'It's not my first time. I've done it with at least fifteen girls till now.'

That ripped off the exclusivity Nityami thought she was serving Aashiq.

'Then, what's the problem?'

'I don't know. I'm not getting sexual vibes from you,' Aashiq said. And he did so in such a casual-rude manner that Nityami became conscious of her nudity. That was it. She quickly put on her clothes and excused herself. That night, she cried a lot.

'Am I not sexually attractive?'

She gave Aashiq another chance a month later, but then too he couldn't get it up. She was even ready for a third chance, but she started sensing that Aashiq wasn't giving her time. Then one day, she saw him singing songs for another girl in the same café where they had met for the first time. After an awkward silence, she left. Nityami had chanced upon Aashiq a year ago at Shopper's Stop. He was working there as a sales executive. It was evident his dreams had gone down the gutter. Nityami didn't know if she should have felt good or bad for him. But by then, he wasn't important enough for her to remember him after she stepped out of Shopper's Stop that day.

* * *

At twenty-four, Nityami met Karan. He was the brother of one of her cousin's friends. They had met during the cousin's wedding. She had never felt an immediate vibe like she did with Karan. From the hour they met, they were on WhatsApp, chatting. Then some more chatting. More and more chatting. They met a few times after the wedding. Everything told her they were simply made for each other. Karan was educated, gentle, wise and practical too. This time, she made him meet her parents as well. They were happy, especially her mother, for Karan was handsome as well. A handsome son-in-law would give her a divine edge over her relatives, she knew.

Though Karan used to work for a software MNC in Mumbai, he used to come down on weekends, which didn't make either of them feel the pinch of a long-distance relationship. Till one day, thirteen months from the day they first met, Karan announced his plans after he secured an on-site opportunity in the US.

'I've not only been promoted but I need to fly to the US in the next two weeks.' Karan's happiness was infectious.

'Wow, congrats. For how many days?' Nityami asked.

'What do you mean how many days? Forever. Who is going to come back to India? Most of my friends are there. The US is the place to be. See, first I'll go. You immediately apply for a visa and resign from your job. I'll be back in two months so that we can get married and together shift there permanently.'

'What will I do there?'

Karan frowned.

'What all my friends' wives are doing. Enjoy the life of the US. Become an Instagram influencer, flaunt your life and be happy with me.'

What hurt Nityami was that Karan had taken a big life decision assuming what her decision would be. Two days later, Nityami told him she wouldn't be able to resign or go to the US. At best, she could travel to Mumbai, taking a transfer from her government job. Karan was shell-shocked. That too told Nityami how Karan perceived her in his head. Sometimes, she wondered, it's surprising that you can surrender yourself to your partner, not knowing the partner has a totally wrong interpretation of your willing surrender to him.

Karan tried to involve her parents. Nityami's mother thought she was being too difficult but her father, though silent, stood by her decision. Nityami wasn't saying she didn't like a domestic life. She would love to play the role of a proper wife but she didn't want to do it going by Karan's rules. She too had some expectations of herself and those were non-negotiable. They remained in touch till Karan came back two months later from the US. To invite her to his wedding. Nityami learnt, during those two months, that his marriage had been arranged, to a girl who was absolutely willing to do what Karan wanted. She was happy for him. But was heartbroken about herself. Deep inside she had imagined Karan would come back and tell her that he understood her point of view and was okay with it. But his love for his career won over his (whatever) love for her.

At twenty-six, she met someone as arranged by her parents. Her mother's sister had brought in the *rishta*, but he turned out to be the biggest loser. Closing the shower tap, as Nityami dried herself, she intentionally didn't think about this one. But when she thought she had seen the worst in guys, in came Raghav when she was twenty-seven. She met him through a dating site.

Nityami stepped out of the washroom, wrapping the towel around her bosom. As she stood in front of the full-length mirror in the room, blow-drying her hair, she wondered why these lessons were being given to her. Why these experiences? Why couldn't Aashiq have turned out to be the way she thought he was? Is this what's called destiny? Whenever Nityami went on a spiralling nostalgia trip, she ended up with more questions than answers. At the end of which she simply couldn't bear any more questions and let life be however it wanted to be.

Nityami quickly got dressed and then went down to have breakfast. As usual, her father was reading the newspaper, sitting by the dining table while her mother was serving him breakfast and waiting for her. She joined them.

'I hope no promotion is coming your way,' Malti Singh Thakur, Nityami's mother, said. Her husband had told her not to nudge their daughter about the OYO room incident any further. She had caught on to another issue to blurt out her frustration.

'Why?' Nityami paused, glanced at her and then continued eating her breakfast.

'Why? Don't you know if you keep rising in your career, then we have to get someone more senior than you to get married to? You know how difficult that is?'

And there was a time when you wanted me to top the class. How confusing parenting can be! Or should it be how convenient? Nityami wondered and glanced at her father, rolled her eyes and focused on her food. Any argument would put her mind in a zone from which peace would be a far cry. Nityami drank more water to push down the paratha, got up and, looking back at her mother, said, 'Of course, mumma, I don't have any promotion coming up. In fact, I had applied for a demotion. I will soon be a peon. I'm sure I'll get a great husband then.' She didn't stop to hear Malti's reaction. Her father, Raghuveer, laughed out loud. Malti looked at him and asked, 'Is she serious?' Raghuveer focused on the newspaper without answering.

If home was not enough, there was her workplace which she loathed even more. Nityami went out, started her Scooty and drove towards her office, preparing herself for the onslaught that her workplace usually brought. Especially on Mondays. And in all this morning rush, Nityami forgot to check her Instagram.

5

It was the usual working day for Nityami. She had studied hard after her graduation and secured a position in INB. Her parents' happiness knew no bounds when her posting was at a branch in Bhopal itself. Nityami was the only one in her college girl gang who had a government position among those who were working. The rest were in the private sector. Some of them had decided to settle abroad. Though Nityami had thought about opting for a private sector job, her parents had explained that only the lucky ones got government jobs. It was their way of sugar-coating their insecurity of living without their daughter. Her mother, in particular, was scared of her daughter falling in love with a *firang* and bearing his babies. Deep inside, Malti was a racist, a sexist, an everything. Though she didn't know it. And didn't care either. Thankfully, her daughter too was happy to be in Bhopal, working as an assistant manager at INB. But Nityami didn't know what kind of hell was waiting for her till she went to the bank on the first day.

The branch itself seemed like it was caught in a time warp. Everything happened in slow motion. The only energetic phase was lunchtime, when every staff member had a smile and excitement on their face. And the moment it was over, they were back to their lifeless-zombie selves. Even during lunch, the conversation the staff had among themselves was something that would make Nityami's ears bleed. Within a month, instead of going to the small space where all the staff used to eat together—all twelve of them except the branch manager who had his own cabin—Nityami decided to stay at her desk with her AirPods on. She listened to her favourite music while munching on lunch. To give an idea of how much the branch was living in the past, Nityami was the only one who had AirPods. The rest had wired earpieces, while half of them had button phones. Not that she judged them because she knew it was just a generational mismatch. But after two months, she did start to judge people purely out of boredom.

Her branch manager, Subhankar Maity, was a pervert. She was sure he used to watch porn in the office since he had extreme mood swings. It seemed that when he couldn't jerk off, he got angry with everyone for any small reason, while there were times when he looked as if he had attained nirvana. Maybe he had jerked out all his semen in one burst then. And this happened quite often, every day. Then there were the three ladies whom everyone called the Aunty Gang. Mrs Singh, Mrs Shah and Mrs Putani. All were past fifty. They had married off their kids and were working only to pass the time, waiting till the bank announced a voluntary retirement scheme when, of course, they would turn the entire branch into a paid kitty party. There was Mr Sharma who worked at the cash counter. He never spoke a single word because his mouth was always full of gutkha. Nityami kept a safe distance from him since she couldn't tolerate the sight of him chewing away. Or the stink of it. The rest of the staff never really bothered about Nityami's presence nor did she register them either.

The average age of the branch staff was forty-five. And Nityami was twenty-seven. On the first day, she stood out simply because of her clothes and styling. She was wearing a salwar kameez, which was more hugging than any that the others had on. It made her feel awkward since she had to endure the long glances not only from some of the customers but also from her seniors. Especially the Aunty Gang. Every day, at different points in time, the Aunty Gang took turns to advise her about fashion, about life choices, ethics and morals, making her feel like she was reluctantly attending a school during her professional life.

Six months later, Hemant Pathak joined the branch as an assistant manager. He was six years older than Nityami. She was happy to have someone who was somewhat on her generation's radar. But the more she talked with Hemant, the more she understood he was not only interested in her but had thoughts of marriage in mind. Nityami wouldn't have minded dating him but there was a major issue that she knew would be a bone of contention for everyone. Truth be told, it was the same for her as well. She was 5 feet 6 inches in height while Hemant was 5 feet 2 inches. And our society wasn't designed in a way where the guy could wear heels and not be mocked. The height was an instant tick-off. Otherwise, Hemant ticked every box. He wasn't handsome but good-looking enough to be a husband; he had no paunch and no receding hairline—two of the most sought-after boxes in arranged marriages after the person's job. Though if the job was big enough, the other two were conveniently excused.

Nityami was given the responsibility of orienting him with the bank and its procedures. While conversing with him, she learnt he was preparing for the UPSC exams, which he had appeared for the maximum times but couldn't qualify for, even though he passed the mains twice in these six years.

'Six years is a long time,' Nityami said. On Hemant's first day, they were sitting chit-chatting over lunch. The mere fact that she had someone close to her age to talk to in the office was an emotional orgasm for her.

'I know. First, it was an aim, then slowly as I failed to convert it, it became stubbornness. It just made me overlook all the practicality of life.'

'You are an engineer, right?'

'Mechanical, yes. But I couldn't have got a job with zero work experience at the age of thirty. So, I chose to prepare for the bank probationary officer exam.'

'I understand.'

'What about you?' Hemant asked. It was the first time someone in her work environment had asked her a personal question.

As the conversations started to happen on a daily basis, a quirky side of Hemant began to peep through. Nityami observed that he used to steer everything to the fact that his future wife would be lucky to have him. Once, he brought bhindi ke pakode for lunch. He shared it with Nityami, who loved it. And instead of a thank-you, what came out was, 'My wife would be happy with me, no?'

Who was this wife? Why did he keep referring to her? Nityami had no idea.

Nityami knew he was a good cook, thanks to the lunch he brought, which he claimed was cooked by him. But the wife thing . . . was it to indirectly lure Nityami?

'Good you don't smoke or drink much,' Nityami had once remarked in the middle of a conversation on addiction.

'I know. I don't have any distractions. Just imagine how much my wife would love it because all my attention would be on her.'

Nityami didn't make it obvious or say it, but she wanted to ask him to see a psychiatrist. From then on, she started avoiding him a bit. Hemant probably understood it. He wasn't a pile-on, but he didn't stop approaching her subtly either.

It had been more than a year since she had been working there. As Nityami took her seat on that Monday morning, she felt frazzled seeing the queue of customers. What had to be attended to the previous day on the personal front now had to be put aside, and she had to be patient with everyone. Sometimes, her frustration convinced her that she should gun down everyone and in the process, she hoped her problems too would be gunned down. But . . . she took a deep breath.

Before starting her work, Nityami thought of checking her Instagram. She hadn't looked at it since the morning. When she tapped the app, it opened to her fake ID as she had closed the app on that profile last night. And she couldn't believe what she was seeing on the screen. Her fake ID followers were at 8819, while the views on her post were 15,345. That was not all. One of the five persons who followed her last was Subhankar. With deepening dread, Nityami clicked on his profile to open it. It was indeed her bank manager. When she checked her own DM next, she saw there were 556 messages, and the message on top was from Subhankar Maity. Sent two minutes ago, she checked. Did he recognize who Naagin Ki Naani was? Nityami wondered, getting a bad feeling about it.

6

Nityami excused herself to go to the tiny washroom. The customer who was hoping his work would finally be done today, after running from one counter to another for fifteen days, abused her in his mind. And then said aloud, 'All they need is a different reason to waste our time. I came here at eight a.m. today so nobody could be ahead of me. And at nine a.m. when work is supposed to start, we have to wait.' He made a face and stood there frowning. Nobody reacted. Nobody cared. Procrastination had become part of the system. The public had accepted it as they had accepted corruption in general.

Nityami locked the door. She could hear her heart beating fast and hard. How the fuck had this one gone viral? she wondered. Was it sheer chance? Or was it her cleavage? Or was it both? And how did it reach her Branch Manager (BM)? And now he had seen 90 per cent of her boobs! Fuck! She exclaimed. Then it struck her that her BM had only seen a pair of boobs, not the person whose 34D they were. Nityami felt weird objectifying her own body parts for the first time in her life. Something that she hated when guys did it. How would she face him? There was a knock on the door. She heard the peon say aloud, 'Madam, Maity sir is calling you. Urgent.'

Was this a bad dream where your fear came alive that immediate second? Nityami wondered and feeling a tight knot in her stomach, opened the door. The peon had left by then, so she went out. While she was walking towards the BM's cabin, the customer who had been waiting since eight a.m. saw her and raised his voice, 'Madam, customers are here. When will you be here?'

Nityami gestured two minutes, made a sorry face hoping the customer would understand her predicament and knocked on the BM's cabin door. The moment she entered, she saw it was the usual scene. Subhankar Maity was cleaning his spectacles, aiming them towards the door. It was always the same. In the beginning, Nityami didn't understand why he was always cleaning his specs when she stepped into his cabin. Then one day she realized Maity used to check the shape of her boobs using his specs as a decoy. And now he had actually seen much more than that. It was just that he didn't know. And she did.

'Sir, you called me?'

'Nityami. Yes. Sit down.'

'Sir, customers are waiting.'

'Customers are customers for that reason. They are supposed to wait. If we give them what they need on time, what would be the difference between a private bank and a government bank?'

'Sir?'

'I mean, five minutes won't kill anyone. Anyway, I called you for two things. One, I have forwarded your name for a seminar to be held in Mumbai. You'll represent the branch there. It will be an all-sponsored trip. Second, you need to help me choose something.'

Nityami was about to feel good about the seminar but the sadness of the second point superseded the joy of the first. This was, she knew, another of his ploys inspired by some B-grade Bollywood movie. He would take her out on the pretext of choosing things for his wife—sometimes it would be rings, sometimes clothes, sometimes just a random gift—and thereby spend time with her. This, too, Nityami had taken time to understand. But by then, she had wholeheartedly helped him, thereby giving him the wrong impression that she was enjoying the outings. When she understood the real reason behind it, she started giving him excuses but the damage had already been done.

'You've been coming with me before, so what happened suddenly?' Maity had asked. A non-confrontational, borderline escapist, Nityami didn't have an answer. Moreover, two years hence she was due for a promotion and the report would go from the BM. All she could do was bring down the frequency of going out with him.

'The day after tomorrow is my anniversary,' Maity said.

'But sir, last year your anniversary was on eighteenth November. How could it shift? Unless you married again?'

'Oh no, I married only once. But this anniversary is of the day we met. Not of our marriage.'

Such a liar, Nityami thought.

'Oh, okay sir. So, what do you want to gift ma'am this time?'

'I was thinking of some kind of necklace. What do you suggest?'

'Brilliant, sir,' Nityami said.

'Great. So, let's go during the lunch hour. We will have lunch somewhere outside.'

'Okay, sir.' Nityami already had a plan. What Raghav had done to her a few days ago was to fan her wrath. And that wrath would now fall on her BM.

Exactly at the start of the lunch hour, Maity messaged her on WhatsApp, asking her to leave first. Then he would. Like always.

'Why do we have to move out separately, sir? We aren't doing anything wrong,' she had asked the first time.

'You're young, Nityami. People are always on the lookout for gossip. Since we aren't doing anything wrong, as you rightly said, we shouldn't be the centre of any gossip either.'

The naive Nityami had believed him then. She felt nauseated thinking of the pettiness of the man now. But she would have her revenge soon, she reminded herself.

Nityami went out and walked to the end of the block. Maity picked her up in his car in the next few minutes. They went to a jewellery store inside a mall. While they were selecting the pieces, Nityami did something she had never done before. Earlier, she didn't want to choose anything expensive unless he asked her to, but he never did. So she used to suggest mid-range jewellery to him. This time she went straight for the ones that cost more than Rs 2 lakh.

'Are you sure? I think this design is a little old,' Maity said quickly, reading the price tag. He could afford something worth up to Rs 30,000, that too in EMIs.

'Of course, sir, I'm sure. Dead sure. In fact, the others are looking dull. It's your anniversary, sir. It has value. The gift too should have value,' Nityami said in her usual innocent voice. Except that her mind knew it was her punch-back time.

'I think you should see some more samples,' Maity said. He couldn't possibly take something worth Rs 2 lakh. Nor could he confess this to Nityami because of his male ego. They spent half an hour in three stores; one within the mall and two outside. But whatever Nityami liked or suggested was above Rs 1 lakh. Maity didn't buy anything, and by the time they were supposed to have lunch, Nityami had called Hemant to the same restaurant.

'Sir, I called Hemant because he got pasta for me today and I didn't eat it. I was feeling bad, being a passionate cook myself, so I thought it would be good to ask him to join us.'

Maity gave Hemant a sombre glance while the latter was full of glee. In the next half an hour, Maity couldn't flirt much with Nityami; he could only sit back and watch Nityami and Hemant converse. He opened his Instagram and messaged Naagin Ki Naani.

Hi, you saw the message but didn't reply. I hope I'm not bothering you.

Nityami had switched on her Instagram notification only after realizing the fake profile had gone viral. As she checked the DM, her heart skipped a beat for obvious reasons. She put her phone back on the table. Maity saw the message had been read. Nityami quickly picked up her phone and excused herself to go to the washroom.

She locked herself in and looked into the mirror. If her life were a film, then this was the moment when she changed from a naive-coy and simple girl next door to the bitch the world deserved. She typed a response and sent it:

Depends. Why should I reply? Give me some motivation.

7

Irrespective of whatever she felt for her BM, Nityami was indeed happy to know her name had been given for a week-long business seminar that was supposed to happen at The Westin, Goregaon, Mumbai. A break was always welcome. Probably, the best thing that Maity ever did for her. The best part was she had to travel alone. Though this was the first time she was travelling alone outside Bhopal, she confided the truth only to her father. Then, together they lied to her mother that she was going with a female colleague. Before take-off, Nityami clicked a picture of the runway in Bhopal and posted it on her real Instagram profile, saying she was excited to travel to Mumbai. By the time she landed, a friend of hers—Nidhi—had DMed her asking her to call her.

Nityami called Nidhi after getting into a cab to The Westin in Goregaon East.

'Why a hotel? You stay with us, no?' Nidhi said. She sounded like she meant it.

'Us as in? Your family is here?'

'Me and Sahil. My boyfriend.'

'You sure?'

'Yeah, else I wouldn't have told you.'

'All right. Let me come after today's session then. Where do you guys put up?'

'Juhu–Versova Link Road. Not very far from Westin. Should take less than an hour for you to reach.'

'Great!'

Nityami checked in to the Westin, freshened up and then immediately went to participate in the seminar. And sitting there she finally understood why her manager must have given her name. It was the most boring session ever. If yawning was a sport in the Olympics, Nityami would have won the gold for India sitting in this session. There were a couple of tea breaks, then lunch and finally the evening tea break. After which Day 1 finally ended. Nityami rushed to her room and then checked out of the hotel with her luggage.

It was a 2BHK that Nidhi and Sahil used to live-in. Nityami knew Nidhi had a boyfriend, especially after she went on and on about his sexual prowess when they had a get-together during Navratri. But she didn't know they were living-in.

'Your parents know about your live-in?' Nityami asked.

'Are you mad? No! They don't even know I have a boyfriend.'

That's why Nidhi never posted any pictures of Sahil on her Instagram, Nityami concluded.

When she met Sahil late in the evening, he looked like the boy-next-door type and not the hunk she had expected. The things Nidhi said he did to her in bed didn't match up with his body type or even attitude.

'Hey Nityami, how are you doing?'

'I'm good. How are you?'

As she continued talking with Nidhi, Nityami also noticed how Sahil went straight to the kitchen and prepared tea for all three of them. When he excused himself to freshen up, Nidhi understood what was going on in her friend's mind.

'We have allocated days between us. We alternate our daily work between us.'

Nityami found that charming. How she wished she was living such a life. At twenty-seven, what was she doing? Giving her mother reasons why she should be a peon rather than an officer!

Sahil turned out to be a great cook. Though he made normal daal-sabzi and a paneer dish, the taste made Nityami ask him, 'Are you a chef by profession?'

Sahil laughed, glanced at Nidhi and said, 'I wanted to be but my family didn't support me. They thought being a chef isn't a cool enough job.'

'How uncool is that! But I understand. So what are you working as?'

'We have an automobile parts business in Indore. I'm handling the Mumbai part of it.'

Nityami loved how effortlessly inclusive Nidhi and Sahil were. She didn't feel any discomfort to slide into their home and stay with them. Though all three used to leave the apartment in the morning, it was only in the evenings they met at home, partied in new pubs listed high on Insta food bloggers' lists, clicked a lot of pictures and came home drunk. Only filtered information was relayed to her parents in Bhopal. Like she told her mother she had done a puja at Siddhivinayak

Temple for a good husband while she was mostly in the trial rooms of Zara and H&M, shopping for herself.

Staying with the couple, Nityami realized living-in wasn't a bad idea after all. She loved what she observed. The inherent trust, the camaraderie, an innate friendship where you could show your true self to your partner, the emotional pampering, the freedom and whatnot. Though she knew of toxic live-ins also, Nidhi and Sahil, thankfully, were different. At night when she retired to her room, the playful moans, grunts and ouches made her blush. Nityami kept imagining what positions they must be trying with a smile on her face. She was happy for Nidhi. Though in that happiness she did sense a certain sadness in her own self. She was twenty-seven and still a virgin. She knew how a man tasted mouth-wise but she didn't know how a man felt inside her. And she didn't like the idea of masturbation. Sometimes, she directed the hand shower in her bathroom below her waist and kept it there till her inner thighs twitched, but that was it. Life in Mumbai was so different from her trapped life in Bhopal that she intentionally stayed away from social media while consuming the moments in the city to the hilt.

The seminar continued to be boring for Nityami. Everyone was at least a decade older than her and she was the only one from her branch, so there was nobody to even catch up with over lunch. She tried to converse with some of the others, but five minutes into it, she realized it was better to put on her AirPods and have her food alone, listening to her favourite music. On the last day, she skipped lunch and called Nidhi.

'Hey, I'm done.'

'So early?'

'It was the last day. Most of the people have already moved out. I think I too shall move out. What's your plan?'

'Let me try and reach home as well then. Let's go shopping,' Nidhi said and the next second added, 'You have the keys, right?'

'Yes. See you soon,' Nityami said. Nidhi had given her a set of spare keys. It took half an hour for Nityami to reach Nidhi's place. When she did, Nityami messaged her.

I reached. You in?

GPS showing 7 more minutes came Nidhi's response.

Nityami thought of freshening up a bit before her friend came. She unlocked the door and entered the flat. Her heart immediately went to her mouth. She saw a naked woman walk in the flat's corridor with a beer bottle in hand. She entered the bedroom. Nityami tiptoed inside, with her heart beating fast, and raised her voice slightly saying, 'Who is inside? Please come out.' Then she added, 'With clothes on.' There was pin-drop silence. A few seconds went by. Nityami took a few steps further inside but was mentally prepared to scoot off if she sensed a violent intruder. You can't trust girls either these days, she remembered her mother's statement. A couple of seconds later, she saw Sahil peep out from the bedroom. He had dressed up haphazardly. The naked woman appeared behind him, now dressed up. Looking as scared as Sahil.

'Nityami, please don't tell Nidhi about this.'

'She . . . she will be here in five minutes,' Nityami managed to speak. She didn't know why she too was feeling scared. Sahil glanced at the woman behind her. She quickly walked passed them and left the flat. An awkward silence followed. Nityami didn't ask Sahil anything. She thought she didn't have the right to. After all, it was Sahil's flat. He too wasn't saying anything. He went inside, and within a minute, came out dressed in another tee and jeans. He too moved out, taking the stairs. Two minutes later, Nidhi stepped on to their floor from the lift.

The entire shopping ordeal followed by coffee was the most claustrophobic outing that Nityami had ever had. Every second she wanted to tell Nidhi what she had witnessed. But the next second she wondered whether she should or not, knowing well what the piece of information could do to their relationship. Nityami kept mum, battling it within her until the night, when Nidhi retired to her bedroom with Sahil while Nityami went to her room. She WhatsApped Nidhi what she had seen and apologized for not mentioning this before. She waited but surprisingly Nidhi didn't reply, even after reading the messages almost immediately.

Even in the morning, Nidhi was quiet. Nityami had a morning flight for which she was ready to leave by 7 a.m. It was only by the main door when Nityami came forward to hug Nidhi that the latter moved two steps behind. She gave Nityami a spiteful glance.

'Do me a favour, Nityami. Never show me your face again,' Nidhi said. Both Nityami and Sahil looked at her. Nidhi looked at Sahil and spoke emphasizing each word, 'She said you were having sex with a girl here yesterday. I mean, I know it's tough to be single but to act in such a way to destroy others who aren't single, is forthright being bitchy.'

Nityami didn't know what to say. Where to look. Or to even clarify. She intentionally didn't look at Sahil, and there was no point looking at Nidhi. Only Nidhi knew why she would react like that. Did she know Sahil was at fault and it was just a defence mechanism to remain blind towards his actions? Did she want to take it up with him in her absence? But then, why would she insult Nityami? Or was it that Nidhi was so scared of breaking things between Sahil and her that she steered the line of blame only to give Sahil a subtle hint that she knew but was still giving him a chance?

Nityami quietly left the flat. Nidhi shut the door with a thud. She would never know what happened inside, Nityami thought, as the lift opened up to take her in. Nityami's first thought when the lift opened on the ground floor was, why the hell did I even come to Mumbai?

8

Nityami tried forgetting the Mumbai episode as a bad dream. The lesson she took from it was she would never stay with a friend who was married or in a relationship. Not while she herself was single. It was after coming back to Bhopal that she opened her fake Instagram profile after a long time.

Naagin Ki Naani was an impulsive act to channelize her inner frustration, but not against anybody in particular. But she didn't know repressed sexuality was an epidemic in India. By the time she came back from Mumbai, she had amassed 27,000 followers. Suddenly, the same Instagram algorithm, which never worked in her original profile's favour, seemed to be infatuated with her fake profile. She'd never seen 3000 messages on her DM. She felt a twisted sense of empowerment. Everyone was asking for Naagin Ki Naani's next reel. Not only that. She had Maity's semi-nude picture without the face which he clicked from the restaurant's washroom and had sent her in reply to her DM response. Nityami couldn't help but laugh for a good two minutes upon seeing the picture.

Nothing eventful happened during office hours. Nityami noticed Maity was constantly messaging and asking for a reply, but she was only 'seeing' the message. The thrill that it gave her, denying someone something, which she had never done before, made Nityami find a new joy in her work. From someone who thought she would always be the one who guys toyed with emotionally, she was now in a space where she could call the shots. The war of the sexes was such a power game, Nityami pondered. And it was important to know when and how you could have leverage over another person.

Before leaving the office for the day, she finally thanked Hemant for accepting her request to come over to the restaurant a week ago.

'I'm sorry. I had to go to Mumbai and I couldn't say this before. Thanks for saving me the other day.'

'No problem. I know office harassment can be quite denting to the self,' he said.

The smile with which Hemant said it made her wonder if she was overjudging him. She knew he had a pretty serious interest in her. One nod from her and they would be dating, if he understood that concept. For the more she interacted with Hemant, she realized he was the old-school type who would make her meet his parents as soon as possible, decide on a date and get married. Then go on thinking he has the girl he loves, but he wouldn't do anything to make her stay with him emotionally. Those everyday acts that make a bond solid. Men generally overlook this after they have the girl they want. Possession is more important for them, not sustenance. In fact, for the toxic ones, possession is the relationship itself. And that was a red flag for her. Apart from his height, which was more of a yellow flag.

'Glad to have a man talk like this,' Nityami said, hoping it wasn't a signal for him to think anything unnecessary.

She reached home from the office and saw that her parents were getting dressed to go out.

'We're going for Rajni's *roka* ceremony,' her mother said.

Rajni was a girl from their locality. Their families were thick. She was two years younger than Nityami.

'Rajni is getting engaged? Why wasn't I told about it? I would have gone shopping for something new. Now I have to wear something old,' she said and noticed her parents exchange a glance. The kind when they weren't sure if they should hide the truth or just say it.

'What?'

'*Beta*,' her father approached her, 'everything happened fast. They had come yesterday and . . .'

'You are lying to me, papa,' Nityami said, with disappointment in her voice. By then, she knew what must have happened. 'You guys go. I'll Zomato my dinner,' Nityami said and took the stairs to her room.

'I've kept some food in the fridge as well.' Her mother said, but by that time, Nityami had locked her room from the inside. Her father didn't like the fact that he had to lie to his daughter, but he told himself it was better than seeing his daughter being humiliated in front of and by people who had known her since she was a toddler. As a father, it pained him to know that he couldn't do much about it either.

After realizing perhaps she was incapable of finding a man for herself, she had given the baton of duty to her parents. It was better that, than hearing her mother's bickering about the marriage matter day in and day out. Little did she know the consequences of this too wouldn't end in her favour. Nityami's social boycott began when her marriage was called off for the second time, after the cards had been distributed. The first time it happened was because the boy had met with an accident and died on the spot while he was driving with his friends to celebrate his bachelor party. The second time the boy pulled out because Nityami learnt he was gay and the marriage was an eyewash. She had to take a stand for herself. And she did. But in the process, she had unknowingly given blind and judgemental society a licence to tag her as an unlucky charm. Her presence wouldn't let other girls get married.

In her room, Nityami broke down. She knew the truth. Nobody loved her presence. She wanted to punch the walls, smash the mirror, tear up her pillows . . . but all she did was take seven deep breaths. She opened Instagram to her fake profile. The notifications told her she was very much wanted there. People were dying for the next glimpse of her.

Nityami stood up, went to her chair, stripped off her salwar and hovered her phone camera over her shapely but thick thighs in a sexy manner, giving a tiny glimpse of her panties as well. Then she uploaded it as her second reel post. By the time the reel was posted on her timeline, she already had on the wicked smile of a vengeful winner.

9

The unreal life within Instagram opened up real thrills and fun for Nityami. She stopped looking at her original profile and spent time chatting with random boys and men asking them, like a queen, to do weird stuff, and they actually did it for her. Some even told her that they were ready to leave their wives for her. Nityami realized how sad that was. The wives must have been thinking how loyal their husbands were and here they were, ready to leave them just because of another pair of 34D and thick thighs. For an instant, even if she wanted to give the men the benefit of the doubt, the situation was still sad. Then a wicked idea occurred to her. She searched for Raghav's profile. His was a personal profile, unlike her fake public one. She found it and sent him a 'follow' request. Within the next half hour, while she was checking her DMs and randomly replying to strangers who were following her, she suddenly got a notification from Raghav not only accepting her follow request but following her back. The next instant, a DM from him also popped up. But Nityami decided to check his Instagram feed first.

She couldn't believe Raghav was already seeing someone. Or so his last two posts said. He was with a girl whom he had tagged on his profile. Nityami checked her profile. Her name was Aabha. That was it. She couldn't see more. She didn't want to. Nityami knew that the more she would see her, the more she would sink into depression. Instead, she thought of replying to his message. She opened her DM, and if she had to check her mirror at that point in time, she would have seen her face resembling the violet devil emoji.

Raghav's message read: *Do we know each other?*

Nityami waited for some time and then typed: *Depends if you know Naagin. I'm her Naani.* She was referring to her user ID. She was satisfied with her cheeky response. Raghav saw the message and responded immediately.

Namaste Naaniji. I know a lot of Naagins actually. Mind specifying?

A smirk later, Nityami replied: *I'm not the one who is in your latest post.*

Raghav answered: *She is my fiancée. But glad it's not you. To be honest, her thighs aren't as sexy as yours.*

'Dog!' Nityami thought and then smiled. The message also validated the fact she was telling herself since the OYO room thing happened. That he didn't deserve her. She couldn't possibly imagine marrying someone who would compare her with a stranger. And then give brownie points to the stranger. It was obvious she wasn't the only profile he was interacting with. Another message came in from Raghav:

I was wondering if thighs were the only thing sexier than hers?

I'm sure I kick balls better, Nityami replied and left the app. She felt anger brewing within her. His was a leading question. Of course, it meant he wanted to see more. Nityami was angry but also genuinely appalled as well. She had not forgiven him for what he had done to her. Invite your would-be fiancée to an OYO room and then assassinate her character with your parents? And now belittling your current fiancée for a girl whose face he hadn't seen? Wow!

Raghav wasn't this on-the-face *tharki*, Nityami thought. Or maybe he was and he didn't show it to her. Sometimes you join the dots only after the passing of a storm. And in that lay your answers. Men who suffer from the pressure of projecting a 'good boy' image in front of the world are the worst.

As Nityami put the phone aside and lay down on the bed, she was lost in thought. She had sent some nudes to Raghav. She wasn't sure if he had deleted them. Her number was blocked by him. So was her original profile. There was no way she could reach out to him. And even if she could and learnt that he had the nudes, it would only be obvious what a bastard he was. What would he be doing with the nudes of, according to him, a character-less girl?

Nityami sat up on the bed. The smile on her face widened as she had a bigger vision of revenge. She picked up her phone again. The DM space between Naagin Ki Naani and Raghav had two messages from him. One was a series of question marks while the next was an emoji of 'I'm wondering'. Nityami typed her reply:

Nothing is for free, mister.

A few minutes later, Raghav messaged:

I'm sorry I can't GPay.

Of course, you can't, you miser. Nityami had paid for the OYO room. This was another time which, when it was happening, she had thought was progressive of him to let her pay for their dates. But later, she understood he was a bloody miser. He seldom paid unless they were having something from a roadside chaat wallah. During her parents' dating days, things were binary. Everything was defined. A man would pay. A woman would enjoy. Now, with women having as much money in their wallet as their partner, it becomes difficult to judge during a date who is coming from a place of equality or a place of being just a miser.

Here, the currency is different.

I'm curious.

What's the worst abuse you have for your fiancée in exchange for a body part of mine?

Nityami assumed he would think for some time but the message came promptly. Raghav was progressively disgusting.

I would say she is a foul-mouthed-self-centred-unnecessarily-rude bitch.

He actually wrote that. He abused his fiancée just for a nude from a supposedly random stranger.

Nityami typed: *She is your fiancée, why do you hate her so much?* Then, on second thought, she erased it. Not so soon, she told herself. She stepped out of bed, stood in front of the mirror, turned and took off her kurta and bra. Then clicked a shot of her back. She shared it with Raghav. He sent seven fire emojis.

Your good name? he asked.

Why do you want to know?

I think with what I saw, I need to say it several times tonight.

Nityami understood what he was hinting at.

I only have a bad name. Naagin Ki Naani.

Naagin is wicked. I'll call you that.

Nityami didn't respond. Less is more, she thought. There was a stupid grin on her face. She went out of her room, down to the dining room. Her parents weren't back yet. With the anger gone and frustration subdued, Nityami was feeling hungry. Zomato would take time so she simply opened the fridge, warmed up the food her mother had left for her dinner and sat down at the dining table to eat. Her phone buzzed with a WhatsApp message.

Up for some ice cream? It was Hemant. She hadn't told him this, but she had been surprised when he asked her what she loved best in Bhopal. After dinner, having ice cream by the lakeside, she said. The last time she had done so was with her parents years ago. The sudden knock on the door of her loneliness made her reply: *That sounds fun. When?*

In fifteen minutes? I can drive down.

After sharing her address with him, she quickly finished her dinner. Hemant was a man of his word; he was waiting outside Nityami's house on his bike exactly fifteen minutes later. She messaged her father that she was going out with a friend and, without caring to read his reply or take his call, sat on the pillion and off they went.

Chit-chatting during the bike ride, Nityami realized how much she needed a friend in life. And maybe, Hemant could be that friend. He was a little absurd at times but he seemed decent. That was all that mattered. They reached the ice cream wallah and Nityami got down from the pillion. She went to check the flavours. Hemant parked the bike and joined her.

'I'll take butterscotch,' she said. Her usual, which she used to order when she used to come there with her parents. Hemant ordered two ice creams of the same flavour. He turned and saw that Nityami had suddenly gone to talk to a group of boys. He followed her, carrying the ice cream cones. The boys went away while Nityami stood still.

'What happened? You know them?' Hemant asked.

'No. I thought one of them was Vedant.'

'Who is Vedant?'

Nityami gave him a sharp glance. Vedant Kaushal was one of those rare people who was nothing to her but at the same time, he was everything.

10

'That's an interesting question.' Nityami said. She was sitting beside Hemant on a cemented barricade overlooking the big statue of Raja Bhoj. There were other families and couples but they were sitting at some distance.

'So, who is Vedant Kaushal?' Nityami had a nostalgic tinge in her voice. Hemant realized the person must have had a deep connection with her.

'He was in my school. My batchmate actually. Our head boy. I saw him for the first time on his first day, which was during our eighth standard. He was standing alone, clueless. I had never seen anyone or anything cuter than him. There was this instant attraction. Not sexual. Or maybe sexual but emotional for sure. Like I wanted to know him. Like a book, which just appeals to you on a visceral level. And you want to read it ASAP. I wanted to know his likes, dislikes, his weaknesses, strengths. His everything. I don't know why.'

'Love, maybe,' Hemant added mildly.

'God knows if we were capable of loving at that time. I was only thirteen or fourteen years old.'

'Perhaps we are capable of loving truly only at that time because we aren't polluted by society. Things are pure within us.'

Nityami threw a sharp glance at Hemant. The truth in his statement hurt her though he had said it casually. The way one says a profound thing without realizing its potential.

'The next four years, which I spent beside him, were the best days of my life,' Nityami continued. 'I don't know how that time flew by. It was also the phase where I was at my stupid best. I used to do weird things. Like, I wrote both our names in a heart sign and stared at it smiling for hours. Every night I hoped I would get to sit close to him during class, or tagged with him in projects.'

'Didn't you tell him about your feelings?' Hemant was finding her story interesting because he could relate to it.

'I didn't. You know, I think some people are born with the talent of secret admiration. That's all they can do. Admire someone with all their heart but from a distance.'

Tell me about it, Hemant thought.

'That was me. Vedant didn't even have a girlfriend. Still, it didn't occur to me that I should approach him. After the twelfth board exams, I thought I would apply to the same college as him but he simply disappeared from everyone's radar.'

'What do you mean, disappeared?'

'His father had a transferable job. This much I knew. And he had come from Lucknow to Bhopal. But where he went after Bhopal is a mystery. He didn't even come to collect his results. At least not on the day when our batch had to. Maybe his certificate was couriered, I don't know.'

'What about common friends? Don't they know where he is right now?'

'You think I didn't try to find out? I asked everyone. The ones close to me, the ones I stayed away from and even the ones I didn't know well in school. Nobody has a clue. I checked social media but he isn't there. A very old Facebook profile is there, but looking at the display picture, I'm certain he doesn't use it at all.'

'Strange.'

'I know.'

'May I ask you something?'

The permission bit made Nityami guess something personal was coming.

'Sure,' she said.

'Why do you still long for him? Is it because it's incomplete? If you had told him your feelings and if he had rejected you, would you still have desired him? It's been so long. Who remembers one's school love for this long?'

'Yeah, it's been nine years since I last saw him. The last time was after our last twelfth standard board exams. He was in our school uniform. He had injured his finger for he had a Band-Aid on his right thumb.' Nityami seemed to be lost in some other world. She came back to the present as a drop of melted butterscotch fell on her hand.

'Why do you think he would have rejected me?'

'If he would have accepted you, we wouldn't be sitting here having ice creams. So, I asked about that situation.'

Hemant had a point. And the more he talked, Nityami asked herself why they hadn't conversed like this before.

'I don't know how I would have reacted if he had rejected me. And to answer your other question as to why I still remember him, it's because I never had a proper and long-time boyfriend. So, maybe he became and stayed as the face to my Mr Right.'

'Hmm, makes sense. Would you still miss him after you get married?'

Now that was a loaded question. And it was because of this trait of his—steering everything towards marriage—that Nityami never saw him as a potential friend outside the office.

'You tell me something first. Why do you have to bring marriage into everything? It's almost like your world revolves around it.'

Hemant laughed, finishing off his ice cream.

'It's a bad habit, I know. But growing up in a small town, my view of a man-woman relationship is unidimensional and limiting. I've tried hard but without the right exposure, I think we remain the way we are from the beginning. Also, the fact that I'm below average height for a man, I think there's something in me that makes me feel I'll lose the person, so let me get married if she is all right with it.'

What caught her attention was Hemant's honesty. He could have easily told her anything else or tried to push his views on marriage on to her, but somewhere he knew where his weakness was and even accepted it in front of a girl. That's rare, Nityami noted. Her phone flashed her father's name.

'Hello Papa, yes I'm on the way, reaching soon.' She ended the call and stood up.

'You know, we should do this more often,' she said.

'Talk about Vedant Kaushal?' Hemant too stood up, dusting his rear.

'No! Ice creams after dinner.'

'I don't mind.'

Nityami went home, revelling in the nostalgia the conversation had triggered. She entered her house, lied to her parents that she was out with a female friend and then went to her room. She didn't even bother asking what had happened at the roka. She lay on her bed and opened Vedant's Facebook profile. She magnified the page and looking at his old display picture where he looked like a college student, asked, 'Where the hell are you? Hemant is right. If I had proposed to you and you had accepted me, we would have been together right now. I know you don't know that. And I also know what I'm doing right now is downright stupid. What the fuck is wrong with me?'

Nityami, with a smile, hugged her pillow tight and closed her eyes to go back in time, to when she had first seen Vedant. And fallen so beautifully, painfully and helplessly in love. She had been living while dreaming about different versions of their school romance from the time she had first seen him. Not for a single night, whenever she had dreams of Vedant, did she not wake up feeling empty inside.

11

In the two or three months that followed, Nityami found herself experiencing new emotions. Feelings she had never experienced before. Thanks to Naagin Ki Naani. With Raghav following her, she blocked Maity from her profile. Not before toying with him a bit.

What a coincidence, even I'm from Bhopal, she told Maity. His obvious reaction was to want to meet her. They fixed a time and a place during work hours.

Bring me some exotic flowers.

When Maity came out of his cabin in the branch with a bunch of exotic flowers in hand, Nityami couldn't stop her laughter. She had to rush to the washroom to laugh her heart out when Maity returned, with no flowers and frustration large on his face. Somewhere she realized the frustration that men had given her so far was given back to them for the first time. She had blocked him then and there.

Her Naagin Ki Naani followers had reached 300K by then, with only ten reels. All, of course, were parts of her body with some ghazal added as background music (BGM) to make it look erotic. She went further and started posting Instagram stories every morning of premium luxury undergarments with a poll asking her followers which one should be her LOTD (Lingerie of the Day). This became a big hit and brought in more followers. The truth was, Nityami had none of those undergarments. She simply took screenshots of them from lingerie websites and posted them as if she owned them. She had understood that teasing a man's mind makes him the most vulnerable. With every reel and each story, she was slowly becoming an ace teaser. Whereas in real life, she didn't have the guts to even wink at a guy from a distance or even strike up a conversation on her own.

Meanwhile, she could feel a nice friendship building up with Hemant. He never came across as someone who was eyeing her body. Or even hinted about sex. After their first ice-cream talk that night, he had also cut down on squeezing marriage into his conversations. That was a relief. The best part was that she could talk about a lot of stuff with him. There was a range. And because there was a range, it never became or seemed boring. Also, they seldom chatted on WhatsApp or did phone calls. It was always a face-to-face conversation. Be it after work hours or sometimes during their post-dinner ice cream sessions.

For a change, Nityami had stopped focusing on what was happening in her friends' lives both on social media and in reality. She understood that if one has things to look forward to in life, one isn't bothered about others' posts on social media. She decided, come what may, she would always keep herself busy. Her alter ego of Naagin Ki Naani was a saviour in this regard. Things were going smoothly when a message from Raghav came as a shock.

Can I make a confession? he asked, DMing her on Instagram.

Sure.

I think I connect with you more than I do with my fiancée.

What are you saying? Nityami was genuinely surprised. Had she been the Nityami of before, she would have gone 'aww' and assumed that perhaps Raghav had realized his mistake. But she was now the Naagin Ki Naani version. She was feeling sadistic joy in Raghav's message, which had pain as a subtext. Though she wasn't sure if he was saying this because he wanted to emotionally manipulate her into meeting him.

I am serious. It's weird but with you I feel free. Actually, you remind me of someone.

Who?

There was a girl. I really connected well with her.

Her name?

Can't name her.

First letter?

N.

Nityami didn't know how to react. She was sure he was talking about her.

What happened to her?

Nothing. My parents didn't like her.

Liar, Nityami thought and typed: *Okay. But do you want to live a life with someone you don't connect so well with?*

My parents like her a lot. So, I'm managing.

Rascal. Men with no spine usually blame it all on their parents. Nityami didn't type this though.

On one hand, Nityami started chatting with Raghav at a more impersonal level while she had a request for Hemant.

'You want me to get in touch with this girl who is your ex's fiancée?' asked Hemant.

'Just to know her side of the story.'

'But how do I do that? Men can respond on DM but it's not that easy with girls.'

'She is a yoga expert. I've done all my research.'

Nityami and Hemant were having their lunch sitting in a space at one side of the office. On the other side, the Aunty Gang sat along with the others. By then the Aunty Gang had assumed Nityami and Hemant were having an illicit affair. Though neither were married, an affair was always illicit according to the Aunty Gang. The ideal woman and man meet the opposite gender via parents, get married and then focus on giving their parents the divine opportunity of becoming grandparents. Once that happens, the couple's existence ceases to exist.

'So, I need to get into her yoga class?' Hemant was diligently trying to understand Nityami's plan.

'It's a win-win. You will be healthier and I'll be wiser about men in general once you tell me what you think of the girl. Her name is Aabha.'

Hemant thought for a moment and said, 'It actually is a win-win.'

It took Hemant one month to become friendly with Aabha, Raghav's fiancée. And his reading of her was that she was too sweet a girl to irk anyone. From the little that he was able to squeeze out of her about Raghav in a casual way, he saw she was all praise for him. Hemant dutifully reported it to Nityami.

'Hmm, I was right. It's the same old my-partner-is-bad-so-I-need-a-shoulder syndrome of a typical Indian male.'

'Don't worry. His karma will get him,' Hemant said.

'Sorry, I can't wait for karma to get him. I would rather be the proxy for karma.'

'What do you have in mind?'

'I want to spare the girl from a lifetime of an ignorant marriage. She will never know what a rascal this person is. Someone who badmouths his fiancée and then posts cosy pictures with her with lovey-dovey captions.'

Nityami had her plan in place but before she could feel the thrill of executing it, there was a notification from her WhatsApp school group. It was a picture invite for an alumni meet of her batch. And the first thing that struck her was: Would Vedant be there?

12

Nityami didn't want to meet the person her mother was suddenly pestering her to, for the last few days. The guy's name was Ishant Singh. He was working with a software giant and was based out of the US. The location did remind Nityami of Karan. But that was not why she wasn't in the mood to meet him. Of late, she had sensed that something was possible with Hemant. The latter didn't tick her boxes exactly but by now, Nityami had understood only the fools wait for the boxes to be ticked. The wise ones alter their boxes with time and simply move on. But she also knew she couldn't introduce Hemant to her family simply because she wasn't 100 per cent sure about him. And she didn't want to give her mother a chance to eat her head asking about Hemant every day and then pushing her to accept him. She wasn't as desperate about her marriage as was her mother. Not yet. And she didn't want to fan that desperation further.

'Can't I meet Ishant some other day?' Nityami asked with a pleading voice.

'No! He is returning to the US next week. He is already meeting girls here. He would share his choice with his parents before he leaves and then come back only for the marriage. So, it's today or never,' her mother said conclusively.

Wow, that's some buffet he has been offered here, she thought and said aloud, 'All right! Where do I have to meet him and when?' Nityami knew that surrendering was the only solution.

It was a mall close to her place. Nityami reached there half an hour before time only so that she could be mentally prepared to meet Ishant. She shopped for some time and then went to try the dresses. Outside the ladies' trial cubicle, she saw a woman and wondered where she had seen her before. The sight of her wasn't pleasing. It didn't let her focus on the dress she was trying on. On a hunch, she moved out and looked out for the lady. It was then that she saw Raghav standing there, busy with his phone, and she remembered who the lady was. Aabha. His fiancée.

Raghav had not seen Nityami till then.

'*Jaan*, come here *na*, please.'

Nityami realized she was in between Aabha and him. He turned and this time Raghav's eyes fell on her. There was a slight twitch on his face—what on earth is she doing here? But Raghav managed it well to cross Nityami and reach Aabha. Not that well though, as Nityami knew he had registered her presence. She stood there unable to move.

'I think it's looking good,' she heard Raghav say. There was a time he had said the same thing and had the same control over her during their short dating stint.

'Are you sure?' It was Aabha. Though Nityami wasn't looking at her directly, she could hear her clearly.

'I'm always sure, jaan.'

The 'jaan' thing was also Raghav's. He used to call Nityami that as well.

'Okay, I'll get this then,' Aabha said. As Raghav turned, he realized he couldn't possibly ignore Nityami. She was the only one standing there and in such a way that much of the space to bypass her was blocked.

As Aabha joined Raghav, he said aloud, looking at Nityami, 'Do I know you?'

Nityami couldn't muster any response.

'Then why are you not excusing me?' Raghav said in a derogatory manner.

Nityami managed to step aside.

'Such fools,' she heard him lament to Aabha as they walked out of the trial space. Nityami's entire body had warmed up. There was a simmering anger within. And ten minutes later, all of it poured out in front of Ishant.

Nityami didn't reply to anything he asked cordially. She was either sarcastic or mean. In her mind, she needed a vent. And both Raghav and Ishant were men. Her mean vent, according to her, was well-directed. The meeting with Ishant lasted fifteen minutes. Ishant was the first one to leave the place where they met. He had not even finished the lemonade he had ordered.

'Please pay for the lemonade and leave,' she said. Ishant did as he was told.

Nityami continued to sit, finished her soft drink and moved out only when she felt a little calm. But that was temporary.

Raghav not only didn't acknowledge her but was rude to her. He insulted her. Till then she had still somewhere given him the benefit of the doubt about the OYO incident. Perhaps his parents had pulled it off on him and he couldn't say no to them. Perhaps! But now it was clear he was as much a rascal as his parents. How she wished she could have punched him in the face. *Do I know you?* Such an asshole!

'I'll show you how you know me.' Nityami hissed under her breath and opened Naagin Ki Naani's Instagram. She went to the DM where she opened the chat with Raghav and left a 'hi'. Half an hour later, Raghav messaged her back:

Sorry was on a call with my fiancée. I would have messaged you tonight.

Why? Nityami replied.

Too horny tonight.

Nityami's jaws were locked as she replied: *How horny?*

Can do anything to see you naked.

Get naked. Tie a tie around your neck. And sit like a dog with your tongue out. Send me a pic. I shall share a complete nude.

Promise?

Get going.

Give me 5 minutes.

Those five minutes were the most sadistic five minutes in Nityami's life. She was imagining all that Raghav would be doing in those five minutes. And while imagining, she also concluded he never deserved her. Men like him, who don't respect women who are ready to do a lot for them, but become lusty dogs for just a little bit of skin, are the men who should be degraded all the time. Around seven minutes later, Raghav's message came in the form of a disappearing image. Nityami didn't open it. She instead replied: *not in the disappearing mode.* It was a command. And it was well taken. Raghav immediately sent her the picture without the disappearing mode on. Nityami laughed her heart out seeing that picture. It wasn't a nude guy trying to be submissive, it wasn't even a reflection of femdom. What made Nityami laugh out was the sheer irony the picture represented. The same girl whom he had character-assassinated along with his parents, the same girl whom he refused to recognize in the mall and then had the balls to insult; now in front of that same girl, he was stripping down his self-respect. She took a screenshot of it. A couple of minutes later, Raghav messaged: *waiting for the full nude.*

Then Nityami sent a gif which said FUCK OFF, SWEETY. Nityami hit her bed with a happy face. But she knew her revenge was not over, yet.

13

As the day of the alumni meet came closer, Nityami pinged almost everyone personally on the school group asking if they had any idea if Vedant Kaushal would come. Nobody knew if he would. One of the boys in the group, who was also on the organizing committee of the alumni meet, told her that the invite had gone not only to the WhatsApp group, Facebook community and their school's Instagram page but also to their addresses as recorded in school. But that wasn't foolproof since Nityami knew Vedant had moved out of Bhopal. The excitement dwindled within minutes. Still, she knew she would go to the alumni meet. If not for Vedant Kaushal at least she would revisit the places she remembered within the school. Each corner had a special memory. And every memory had Vedant in it.

Nityami told Hemant about the alumni meet during one of their post-dinner ice cream sessions.

'When was the last time you went to the school?' Hemant asked. This time they were having a strawberry-vanilla mix flavour.

'I've passed by many times but never went inside,' Nityami said.

'Same. Been years since I went to my alma mater even when I was in my home town. Anyway, would you meet Vedant if he came?'

'Of course.'

'And will you propose to him?'

'If he isn't married, I may.'

'But won't it look creepy? No connection for nine years and suddenly a proposal?'

'Are you trying to discourage me?'

'A part of me doesn't want you to be committed. I don't know why, I'm now feeling jealous of Vedant.'

Nityami gave him an 'Are you kidding me?' look.

'Committed to him or anybody in general?' Nityami was leading him now.

'To anybody in general,' Hemant said, without looking at her.

'Are you saying you are interested in me romantically?'

'I thought you knew that but intentionally ignored it.'

'That's because I can't get closer to someone with marriage on his mind. In that case, I would look at you only through the lens of whether you are a marriageable guy or not. I may miss the person you actually are. And it would be the same for you.'

'If we take the marriage thing out, can we date?' Hemant sounded excited. It made Nityami smile. Did he just ask her out?

'Maybe,' she said.

'Don't be ambiguous here, please. I don't want to be the guy who, after ten years, would tell my future wife that I liked a girl but her response was ambiguous. Like you are telling me about Vedant.'

Nityami laughed out loud.

Though she didn't tell Hemant anything about her Naagin Ki Naani avatar, she shared everything else during those two hours of conversation. So did he. They were in an official relationship from the next day onwards. The difference in behaviour between them told everyone in the office what was brewing. The most jealous was Maity, who couldn't bear the thought that the girl he was eyeing was being enjoyed by Hemant in bed. Maity's thoughts were always triggered by his little balls rather than his brains.

Ten days later, Nityami made Hemant meet her parents. Her mother made it seem to Hemant as if his home visit was a *Kaun Banega Crorepati* (KBC) quiz as she kept darting out one question after the other. The top and only prize was, of course, Nityami's hand in marriage.

Mrs Thakur's plan for her daughter was different though. She never took her daughter's job seriously. She thought they would get a guy who had the possibility of shifting to the US. Or anywhere abroad. Her daughter would leave her job then and enjoy her life there. And a few times, Mrs Thakur would also go with her husband to visit their daughter in the US. But Hemant had no such prospects. After he left, her mother also mentioned his height to Nityami.

'I know, Ma, he is shorter than me but then what do you need? Your daughter's happiness or whether she is the shorter one?'

'Happiness comes from a successful career.'

'Ma, Hemant works in the same organization as me. Are you saying I'm having a disaster of a career?'

Her mother was quiet for some time and then said, 'It's different for a girl.' Nityami couldn't take it. She threw a disappointed glance at her father who was about to say something to pacify the situation but by then Nityami had walked out on them.

Her pissed-off self pushed her to post another reel on her fake profile. Her fifteenth. As it started receiving likes and comments, she realized Raghav had been inactive for a few days. When she visited his profile, she noticed his story had a date announcement video. He was getting married. They hadn't been chatting since he shared the nude with her. It was time for her to put her final plan into action.

Nityami took screenshots of the chat between Raghav and Naagin Ki Naani, and DM-ed Raghav congratulating him on his upcoming marriage. He, in turn, messaged back saying he felt lost since his heart wasn't in the marriage. Nityami asked if he wanted to meet.

I missed you so much these days. I thought you were ignoring me. So, where do we meet? Raghav asked instantly.

Oyo room. I'll DM you the address and time, Nityami messaged back.

14

Nityami took a printout of the entire chat between Naagin Ki Naani and Raghav. From the first day till the present. She put the pages inside an envelope and the next day, left it outside the yoga studio where Raghav's fiancée, Aabha, taught. The chat also had the OYO hotel address where Raghav was supposed to book a room and meet Naagin Ki Naani in person. For the first time in Nityami's life, everything had happened as per plan.

Raghav was waiting for Naagin Ki Naani to arrive at the hotel. He was there on time, waiting. Just like the day he was waiting for Nityami. Except his parents weren't with him this time. When there was a knock on the door, Raghav opened it with a smile. Then stood frozen.

'I'm here for work, baby,' Raghav managed to say but by then, Aabha had hurled the printouts at him. There was a momentary eye-lock. Raghav could see that he had fallen badly in her eyes. She dashed off with moist eyes. As Raghav picked up the printouts and realized what those papers were, he couldn't fathom why Naagin Ki Naani would send them to his fiancée. Who was she, really?

A day later, when she noticed that Aabha had unfollowed Raghav and he had removed all their pictures from his feed, Nityami knew that her revenge was fruitful. She wasn't repentant one bit that she had broken a relationship. For it wasn't one. The girl only thought it was while Raghav was simply making a fool of her.

Satisfied on the one hand, Nityami continued her newfound relationship with Hemant. It was the friendship with him that was more alluring. And every time he brought up the subject of making their respective parents meet for once, she wondered if the friendship would survive their romantic relationship. She had grown up hearing a boy and a girl can't be friends. But what if they were? Would it make their love life, when they step into it, suffer? This was never addressed anywhere.

Hemant, on the other hand, seemed clearer about his wants. Talking to him, Nityami got the vibe he was sure he wanted her as his wife. Because of his promise to her, he didn't bring up the subject of marriage, but there was a sense of clarity in him that was troubling her. Troubling because she wasn't certain. She knew they were dating, but her idea of dating Hemant was to know if he was the one while he saw the dating phase as a bridge to marriage. They were on different pages. Was she not clear because of her past experience or was it because she was still in love with someone else deep inside?

A few weeks later, the school alumni meet happened. The dress code was casual. Nityami dressed up in ethnic wear. Hemant dropped her off at the school. The school auditorium was turned into a buffet dinner space. Most of the old teachers were there. Nityami met them first, one by one. Their happiness was more in meeting those students who had settled down in life. By settled, it meant the ones who were married and had kids. The same teachers who had once taught them not to be biased or judge people were themselves prisoners of the vice.

With an eye out to see if Vedant was present or not, Nityami decided to meet her other batchmates. In comparison to the girls, there were more boys in the meet. Most of the girls of the batch, as she learnt, were out of India. Only one girl from her girl gang was present. As everyone started catching up, discussing the old crushes, memories and flings that had happened in school, Nityami, at one point in time, detached herself from the group and left the auditorium.

Though the school premises were empty of students, she could hear the buzz in her mind. The hubbub of a normal school morning. She could see students moving around and somewhere near the assembly space, she could see a teenage girl waiting with bated breath to catch a glimpse of her first love. She did that for four years without a break. Where had those days gone? Nityami almost felt like crying. And she did. If someone had told her she would not get a glimpse of Vedant after school ended, she would have surely proposed to him. Or at least exchanged emails or numbers or addresses. Just to be in touch with the person who had taken her on such a beautiful journey inside her. Nobody told her it would never happen again, for innocence is lived once. Lost once. There's no return to it ever again in life.

She felt someone's presence nearby. As she turned, she noticed it was Ankit, a boy from her batch. He was the one who was the most unrecognizable, with a bald patch at that young age.

'You all right?' he asked.

'Yes.' Nityami got a grip on herself. Ankit was someone she didn't even remember much from her batchmates. Pretty much an invisible personality back then.

'You're the one who was looking for Vedant, right?' he asked.

'I was, yeah.'

'I saw your message on our school's Facebook community. I thought I would tell you face to face.'

Nityami came up to him. There was a sense of eagerness in her.

'You know where Vedant is?' She asked.

'Gurudongmar Lake.'

'Sikkim? But who stays there?'

'Not staying. He's been camping there for the last three months. I met him in May. It's June now. So he must still be there.'

'Oh. Any phone number?'

'He said he didn't use one. Nor does he use much of social media. Weird!'

He was always different from the others, Nityami thought and asked, 'Is he . . . married?' She immediately realized she shouldn't have asked it.

'No. In fact, I thought he was dating you.'

'Dating me?' Nityami couldn't believe what Ankit was saying. Or was he simply being a jerk?

'He mentioned your name.'

What. The. Fuck. Vedant Kaushal mentioned my name? Fuck. The. What. The. Fuck.

A week later, Nityami was on a flight to Bagdogra from where she was supposed to hail a cab and go upwards till she reached Gurudongmar Lake. She told her parents there was an office seminar for a week in Kolkata while to Hemant she said there was a distant relative's marriage because of which she was flying to Kolkata. Only she knew how little she had slept after knowing that Vedant had mentioned her name. Leave that aside. The fact that he wasn't married and that she had his location was an opportunity of a lifetime that she couldn't let go of. And it had come at the right moment, when she had to choose whether to be friends with Hemant or accept him as a life partner. For once, she was happy for all those guys who had rejected her.

Nityami's flight landed on time. She took her luggage, called both her parents and Hemant, lying to them that she had reached Kolkata safely and then went out to see a guy carrying a placard with her name. It was her driver. She waved at him. He came forward, took her luggage and sprinted ahead. She followed him until she reached the cab, an Innova.

As she settled down, she noticed the driver had kept her placard on the dashboard and had taken up another one.

'What happened? Why are you not driving?'

'Madam, going to fetch another passenger. The flight is arriving in ten minutes.'

'Oh. There's another booking?'

'Yes. There's another madam flying in.'

'Madam who?' Nityami asked.

GIRL TWO

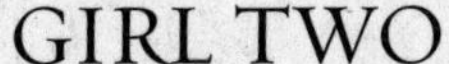

1

There were sixty students in all in the MBA first year of Bharat Institute of Management, New Delhi. The college wasn't the numero uno one. In fact, it ranked forty-first that year amongst all the MBA institutes in India. And it didn't even require a high CAT score. But apart from that, Falak Sultana was ecstatic when she got the admission call email. For her, it wasn't just an admission call email but a call to freedom.

She was in the third semester of her first year currently. The students were divided into six groups of ten each, with names Team A to Team F. Each group was to choose a topic and come back after the Diwali break with a presentation. Falak was in the E group. And they had collectively chosen to present the market analysis of a newly launched toffee, which was on the upswing sales-wise in a highly competitive market. Once the team had divided the work amongst themselves, they started discussing their Diwali plans.

Everyone had a plan. Except Falak. Not because she wasn't a Hindu. She never had plans for Eid either. Hearing everyone talk about their plans and their families, Falak thought how blessed her team members were to have a normal family. In all the twenty-two years of her life on earth, Falak had understood it was all about which family you were born into that determined half of where you reached. The family one is born into, Falak realized, was like the extent of the stretch of one's life's catapult. The longer the stretch, the further the projectile flew. Unfortunately, she was born in the middle of a hurricane. And for Falak Sultana, it was only her non-negotiable stubbornness that made her reach where she had in life.

Unlike her batchmates, she had grown up with a hunger for securing a human's basic needs at a daily level. Her fight wasn't about why her BFF left her or why she had to compromise on Gucci and wear Zara instead. Her fights were about, will I be able to eat three meals today? Will I be able to study? Will I be able to earn an identity for myself? Will I be able to escape being a sexual object for an elderly man sometime in the future? The everyday fight was dark but never for one day did Falak let the light in her, something with which she was born, ever flicker. By the age of ten, she understood that the light was everything she had. And if she compromised that because of life's storms, then she would be like everyone else around her. Animals who called going about fetching food for oneself a life. Mere existence. Falak didn't want to exist, she wanted to *live*. Live a life without being worried about securing her basic needs. She clearly remembered that night when the thought had perched in her mind for the first time when she was ten.

Her father had come home drunk, and after two steps, collapsed on the floor of the small space that they told everyone else was their home. Falak didn't bother to probe him. Her mind was somewhere else. There were only three pieces of bread at home. Even though she was of a tender age, it was her duty to serve her father and brother when they came back from work. Her brother, Imtiaz, was sixteen at the time. When he came home, an hour after her father, Falak knew neither her father nor her brother had brought any food for the night. And if her brother got to know there were only a few pieces of bread left, he would eat it all. When Imtiaz went to the common bathroom outside to freshen up, she followed him stealthily, then locked him inside the common bathroom. She quickly came back to finish the bread.

Someone in the locality opened the door when Imtiaz started banging it. When he came back, Falak told him there was no food. Irked, he slapped her for not telling him before, then went out with his friends. Falak didn't mind the slaps for she knew she would sleep with a half-full stomach. This was the first time she learnt that sacrifice was a vice if you do it for those who never appreciate it. This was also the night she promised herself she would always keep her home full of food. For where there was food, there was contentment.

The MBA group dispersed as the day got over. The day scholars went out while the hostel dwellers took another direction within the campus. While Falak was walking out of her classroom, she was stopped by the marketing professor.

'How are you doing, Falak?' said Professor Abhijit Gupta.

'I'm fine, sir. Thanks for asking. Also, happy Diwali.'

'Any plans?' he asked, as if he already knew the answer but still wanted to hear it from her.

'Not really.'

'I was actually noticing you when the others were discussing their plans.'

Abhijit was not just a professor for the students but donned many hats when it came to them. Sometimes he became their friend, sometimes a mentor and at times, their secret keeper.

'I know your story, Falak.'

There was a moment of weakness for Falak. She thought he would sympathize with her. And she didn't know where she should hide herself for Falak could take a lot of pain but not an iota of pity from anyone.

'You are different from the others,' she heard the professor say. Those weren't the words she was expecting.

'I say this from experience. I have taught many batches here but rarely have I seen someone as determined as you. Do you know the basic difference between you and the others here?'

'Maybe I come from a humble background,' Falak said with a slight shrug, only to see the professor shake his head in disagreement.

'There are three words that make you different from the others here and perhaps from many outside too. Students here know where they need to go in life. While you know where you need to go in life, come what may. Those three words . . . come what may . . . that's the difference.'

Abhijit Gupta was spot on. Falak knew she could take pride in it but there was a lurking fear too, which she sensed within.

'But those three words, sir, make the rope I walk on every day very thin compared to the others.'

'It definitely does, but it also makes your focus sharper. The thinner the rope, the sharper the focus. Which tells me your chances of making it to where you want to go are higher than the others. Not that it's a comparative race but since I observed you were getting a little bogged down, I thought you must know this.'

Subconsciously perhaps, she always knew but she needed someone to tell her that. It was like an encouraging pat on the back.

'I can't thank you enough, sir,' Falak beamed from ear to ear.

'Consider this a Diwali gift from my end. Happy Diwali to you too.'

Falak gave him a hopeful smile. As Professor Gupta took his leave, she heard her phone ring. It was from an unsaved number. Moving out of the class with her laptop bag, Falak took the call. It was a short one but it validated something she had grown up believing about herself. For every smile of hers, life would throw a fight at her. And from whatever she heard on the call from the Delhi police officer, she knew a fight was waiting.

At least now she knew how her upcoming holiday would go.

Like shit.

2

Falak Sultana, on her boyfriend Wasim's bike, was riding to her clients one by one, to whom she used to send tiffin on a daily basis.

'I'm in some kind of crisis. Can you please clear the dues for this month now itself?' It was the same thing she told all her clients. Some obliged, some didn't. Thankfully, the number of people who gave her the money in advance was in the majority.

Cooking had been Falak's passion since she was thirteen. Turning to cooking for pocket money at twenty-three was more of a compulsion than a desire. She quickly counted the money she had collected from her clients and headed to the police station. The lawyer was supposed to meet her there. Wasim had been taken into custody—for the umpteenth time—for instigating some of the students in the university. Whether it was true or not wasn't the point, really. Not for Falak at least. When she reached the police station, after she'd received the call, all she cared about was how much money was needed to bail Wasim out. The reason why he was being held by the Delhi police was a stale one.

Falak reached the police station a little late but she had already messaged the lawyer to wait. He did. Not for her. But for the money she was giving him for getting Wasim bail. Of late, Wasim had become the lawyer's regular client. All of the police staff also had come to know Wasim. When Falak entered the police station, she noticed Wasim playing cards with a couple of constables and laughing over some joke. She didn't say anything, just locked her jaw. She waited till his bail was done by the lawyer to whom she gave not only his fees but also the bail amount.

Once she was out with Wasim, and they were heading to his bike, she said, 'How many times do I need to tell you I can't go on bailing you out because of your stupidity?'

'Student activism isn't stupidity. You won't get it.'

'Activism my foot. For whom is this activism? You were a good student; couldn't you have taken up a job? Earned for yourself? Lived away from police stations and lawyers? And given me some peace?'

Wasim stared at Falak and then slapped her hard saying, 'Don't ever tell me what I should do or shouldn't.'

He was about to get on the bike when Falak stopped him. He turned and before he knew it, Falak had kneed him in the balls. Wasim grabbed his groin and dropped to a hunched pose, screaming abuses against her.

'Never talk to me like that,' Falak said. She kicked him again. He collapsed on the ground. She got on his bike and started it. Looking at Wasim, she said, 'Come home on your own. And if you don't remember, just know that nobody is waiting either.'

Falak drove off. She went back home, studied and made notes while yawning continuously, since she had been up all night chopping vegetables and marinating chicken so she could cook them quickly in the morning, prepare the tiffin boxes and also deliver them herself. A little later, her stepmother, Razia, stepped in and offered her something sweet.

'I know how much you like sevai. I made it fresh,' Razia said.

Falak hugged Razia tight. Though Razia was her stepmother, she was also her best friend. After all, the age difference between them was just one year. Razia was also the only good thing that had happened to her.

In fact, she was the second-best thing. The first was named Vedant Kaushal.

3

Life for her was as complicated as life could be, but Falak Sultana always had a simple way of looking at it: problems are overrated. She was born to Mohammad Zamaan and Amina. They lived in a chawl in Bandra East in Mumbai. Amina died after giving birth to three sons and then Falak. Zamaan used to work as a driver for a Bihari bhai who had five SUVs that he floated as cabs for a call centre. He usually had the night duty of picking up employees from their homes and then dropping them off at the office. And in the morning, the reverse. He worked diligently to take care of his family. The eldest son eloped when he was seventeen to somewhere nobody knew. Nor cared. The second son, Imtiaz, was responsible enough; Zamaan taught him to drive and then took him on as a driver in the Bihari bhai's cab service. Over time, the business expanded to provide tourist cab services to Shirdi, Karjat, Panchgani, Alibaug, Goa and other places. The third son died of typhoid when he was eight. Falak, under the careless tutelage of two men, grew up to be a rebel. Not that she had any other option.

She realized early in life that whatever she wanted wouldn't be given to her since she was a girl. She wanted education. She wanted to earn. She wanted to make her life decisions herself. Zamaan had got her a job washing utensils at a nearby place so the money she brought in could pay his alcohol bills. Unlike a true Muslim, he had all the bad habits of drinking alcohol, going to prostitutes, smoking weed. Ravikant Mhatre, in whose home Falak used to wash utensils, was a teacher in a private school. When she told him she wanted to study, he made sure he not only taught her but also put her in a government school, seeing her sharp mind. He had a lot of jack so Falak had to pay no fees. In front of Zamaan, his daughter would act all dumb and docile, but when he wasn't around, she slowly shaped up into a tigress who knew what she wanted.

Falak passed her school examinations with flying colours and enrolled herself into one of the famous colleges of Mumbai for her BCom. It was during that time Zamaan ended up helping to save a distant cousin's life in Delhi. They needed Rs 2,50,000 for a surgery and Zamaan provided it overnight, taking a loan from the Bihari bhai. In return, he asked his cousin for his daughter's hand in marriage. The cousin wasn't in a position to say no, but his only request was for her to be allowed to stay in Delhi for some time till he got well completely. The doctor had given him three months to recuperate. Zamaan agreed only after his cousin told him that all his train tickets between Mumbai and Delhi would be paid for by him whenever he wanted to travel. As Zamaan started going to and fro, he realized this was the perfect set-up for him. He didn't marry Razia because he needed emotional support. It was sex. He needed legit sex. And he was tired of the tag of a widower. After visiting her a few times, he discovered he could fuck Razia when in Delhi while in Mumbai there was no pressure of domestic life at all. He was fifty-five and she was twenty-four. There was nothing they could talk about or relate to in each other. Truth be told, Zamaan hadn't seen Razia properly either, except for her photos.

It was during the *walima* that Falak realized her stepmother was her age. And as they stayed in touch, Razia realized that Falak was everything she wanted to be in her fantasies. She was educated, a degree holder, pursuing a professional course and earning for herself. It was only Razia who supported her when Falak told her she had cracked an MBA entrance.

'But my MBA college is in Delhi. Abbu will never allow me to shift to Delhi,' Falak said over a video call with Razia. The latter thought for some time and then said, 'Leave it to me.'

'What will you do?' Falak was curious. The next time Zamaan visited Razia in Delhi, a week after the video call with Falak, she did something to him she had never done before. She gave him an ethereal oral during their sex. And it was so unprecedently orgasmic for Zamaan that she made him promise, in the name of similar pleasure moments in the future, that he would grant her whatever she wanted.

'Can Falak stay here with me?' Razia asked as Zamaan fell on top of her after coming inside her. He wasn't using any protection but Razia kept a pill ready without telling him.

'Actually, when I have a stepdaughter, I might as well make some use of her here at home,' she added.

Zamaan was in some other world. He could still feel Razia's tongue on his dick. And the thought of it made his placid dick twitch.

'I don't mind,' he said. Anyway, Zamaan never knew what to do with Falak. First, he thought that after three sons, he would have another boy. Then he thought she would take care of the house after her mother's demise. That didn't happen. Whatever Zamaan expected out of Falak never happened. She was more a grain of sand in his eye than some treasure. On top of it, she was quickly getting to the marriageable age, which would mean further expenses.

Falak couldn't believe Razia had pulled it off, and Razia never told her how she did it. Though they were almost of the same age, Razia couldn't possibly disclose certain intimate details. For the last year, Falak had been in Delhi, pursuing her MBA and earning by preparing tiffin for clients.

Wasim came into her life two months into her shift to Delhi. Falak knew she would need one guy who would keep other unnecessary guys away. He was more of a necessary evil for her, which she knew she couldn't possibly negate. Thus, she endured him. She wasn't in love with him one bit. But when Razia had told her that her Abbu was thinking of letting Wasim become her future husband, she knew it was only better to keep him closer to her so she got used to him. Life, Falak always observed, was so much about getting used to things. Even if those things weren't what you were comfortable with. Comfort, after all, was also a state of mind. Especially for people like Falak. Wasim was the son of one of Zamaan's distant cousins. It meant he would always be on her radar.

Falak didn't have any problem with Wasim in particular, except she knew he had to sort his shit out. Yes, he was abusive. Yes, he didn't respect her. Yes, he was forever condescending towards her no matter what she did for him. But that was a norm with men. Or at least the ones she had seen in close proximity. At thirty, Wasim was neck-deep in student politics. She prayed that the Almighty would give him enough sense to see that all this would not lead anywhere. And that this was, at best, a delusional tomfoolery he was involving himself in. Not that she cared for him. She wanted to reduce her post-marriage problems. But Wasim was still pursuing student activism because of his loyalty towards a Muslim MLA, who had promised him and guys like him god knows what. Not that Falak was this heartless when it came to relationships. When she was doing her BCom in a Mumbai college, she met a guy during an inter-college fest. The fest ran for a week, and she met him over five days and fell in love with him forever.

Vedant Kaushal wasn't just a name for Falak. It was a place within her that introduced her to pleasurable pain, happy tears and painful pleasure. All at the same time.

4

Though Falak never, even once, asked Razia to accompany her whenever she went to the market, either to buy veggies, fish and meat for the home or for the kitchen she ran for her clientele, the latter always joined her the moment she crossed her house lane.

As the two ladies were en route to the vegetable market nearby, Falak told Razia about the kind of work pressure she was under because she had taken some advance money from a few clients to bail out Wasim.

'Initially, I thought I would rest for two days, now that the institute is also closed but I can't.'

'I won't lie,' Razia said, 'but I always wonder why Wasim? I know the reason you told me earlier. That you need a guy to keep other guys away. And that eventually you fear you would be married off to him since he is on your Abbu's radar. But seriously, why him? Are these reasons even worth Wasim?'

Sometimes, Falak walked ahead of Razia because of the busy road. Falak answered only when they were finally walking shoulder to shoulder.

'I think it's the scenario of a known devil being better than an unknown one.'

'Devil nevertheless.'

'You think we have a prince in our destinies otherwise? Like if I had not chosen Wasim, I would have the best man on the planet for me?'

'I'm not saying that. If not the best, maybe not as bad as Wasim? Maybe more sensible. More sensitive.'

Falak didn't answer immediately but Razia knew she was thinking about it. They entered the vegetable market first. Falak went to the vendor from whom she used to buy veggies regularly.

'Vikas bhai, aloo, tamatar, bhindi, gobi, pyaaz, sab ek ek kilo,' Falak said as she hovered her eyes on the paper list she was carrying first and then on the vegetables on display in front of her.

'Behen, pehle ka hisab bacha hai,' Vikas informed her about her past credit.

'Haan, de dungi.' Falak was always late but she did pay nonetheless.

'Woh toh pata hai.' Vikas had a warm smile on his face. *'Main bas bata ke rakh raha tha.'*

As Vikas got busy sorting the veggies for Falak, the latter turned to Razia and said, 'Wasim, in all honesty, is a temporary plan. I hadn't gotten admission to the MBA when I boyfriend-ed him. Now I have my plan clear.'

'Which is?'

'To clear the MBA, secure a job and ghost-out from his life.'

'What if he tells your Abbu about the living-in, the sex?' Razia kept her voice low while speaking.

'Then I'll mix rat poison in their roti and kill them,' Falak said. For a moment Razia, looking at her, didn't understand if she was kidding or serious. She relaxed only on seeing Falak burst out into laughter. Razia relaxed.

'I thought a lot, Razia. I can't compromise my life because of these men. Or any man for that matter. I'll ghost not only him but Abbu also. You think I'll be in touch with him once I secure a job?'

'Does that mean you'll not be in touch with me also?'

'Oh come on, Razia. You're my soulmate.' Falak gave Razia a hug.

'I wish I could also say your Abbu was a temporary plan for me.'

'He can be.'

'Really? How?'

By then Vikas had handed over the packets with the veggies. Falak asked him to add the total to her credit and then they turned to go towards the mutton shop.

'It's simple. Once I leave Delhi, you go and live with him in Mumbai. Make him drink as much as possible. You're just twenty-three. Even if you make him drink for seven years, his liver will be destroyed. He would die. Then you are free. And at thirty years, women are at the peak of their sexual health.'

'Shut up!' Razia said and looked around quickly to check if anyone had heard them. Nobody seemed bothered.

'Why are your ideas so violent? Can't we do things without killing?' Razia asked.

Falak glanced at her and said, 'Our starting point has been extreme, thus the cost of our freedom will also be extreme. There's no midway, Razia sweety. You think if I had taken the midway of asking or trying to convince Abbu that I want to pursue a corporate career or a business of mine, he would have said yes?'

Razia's silence was a confirmation that what Falak was saying was the truth. They remained quiet as they reached the mutton shop. Razia too bought a little for herself and her ailing father. Once they were handed over the black packet that contained the chopped mutton pieces, Falak glanced at Razia and asked, 'Leave all this. There's no end to it. Now tell me, what's the plan for midnight? It's your birthday tomorrow.'

Razia's face told her all. There was no plan.

'Just be outside your gate at 10 p.m. tonight,' Falak said.

'Wait. What are you planning?'

'It's a surprise, Razia sweety.'

And Razia knew she should be worried.

At nine at night, Falak made the best mutton curry there could be. She served Wasim, who ate so much that he soon felt sleepy. Little did he know that Falak had googled over-the-counter sleeping pills and had mixed a sizeable amount in the bowl of mutton curry for Wasim. Seeing him snore away in the bedroom, Falak locked the room and then drove off on his bike to Razia's.

'Where's Wasim? What's happening?'

'Fun.' Falak said and promised her that she would tell her everything but later. They reached a nearby mall. Falak showed Razia tickets for a night show of a recently released

Shah Rukh Khan film. Both were die-hard SRKians. But before that, Falak made Razia put on a new outfit, which they bought in the mall itself. Clicked several photographs. They ordered their food in the cinema hall itself. And during the interval, as it was midnight, they went to the security guards who had kept Razia's cake with them. They cut it there with the security officers too joining in. Then they rushed back to the hall to finish watching the film. It was 1.30 a.m. when the movie ended and they moved out of the hall. As Falak rode her bike with Razia on the pillion, the latter got emotional.

'Thanks, Falak.' She kissed her nape from behind. The bike immediately wobbled.

'Arrey, I'm driving. This tickles me.'

'This was the best birthday I have experienced.'

'Did Abbu message?' Falak asked.

'Does he even care? Nobody cares, Falak. And that's what our injuries are all about. Nobody cares because nobody respects our existence. Everything about us is taken for granted. Every-goddamn-thing.'

Falak only wished she could refute it but she knew it was true.

'Tell me,' Falak didn't want Razia to be sad on her birthday so she changed the topic, 'What's the craziest thing you ever did, Razia sweety?'

'Marry your Abbu.'

Both laughed out as the bike sped on the lonely Delhi road.

'My life is uneventful. I was born, I existed and now I'm married. That's all.'

'You want to do something memorable?'

'I can already feel my stomach churn. Please don't tell me you have something naughty in your mind.'

'Do you remember the guy who was standing in the popcorn line during the interval after we cut the cake?' Falak asked.

Razia frowned and said, 'The one who was checking me out even though he was with a female?'

'Yes. The one whom you too were checking out.'

Razia blushed. 'Nothing escapes you, right?'

'Now, question number two. Did you realize we aren't on the usual road to our home?'

Razia immediately looked around, 'I thought you knew another route.'

'Now, the third. Can you see a car a little ahead of us?'

'Yes,' Razia said, noticing a Hyundai Creta ahead of them.

'So, now let me connect the dots for you. That guy by the popcorn counter is driving it and his girl is sitting beside him.'

'How do you know she is his girlfriend? Could be a female friend also?'

'Razia sweety, nobody smooches a female friend in the theatre.'

'They did that?'

'Forget that. Now tell me, do you want to do something which we will never forget?'

'I'm not liking it,' Razia said in an intrigued manner. The contradiction in her words and tone made Falak smile.

'I'm going to drive the bike fast past the car. And I dare you to give him a flying kiss and a middle finger to his girlfriend. Are you ready for a sin, Razia sweety?'

Razia could feel a hundred butterflies in her stomach. She did check the guy out but that was beside the point now. She could feel a nervousness brewing in her.

'Ready? One . . . two . . . and . . .'

On the count of three, Falak sped her bike and came parallel to the car. The guy noticed them. Then the bike went ahead so Razia could turn. She did. And then did what Falak dared her to. Except she ended up showing the middle finger to the guy and gave the flying kiss to the girl.

Falak sped away, taking a left from the Y road ahead while the Creta took the right. They heard the girl in the car scream out loud, 'I love you too!'

When Razia clarified why the girl had done that, Falak laughed aloud saying, 'Now even I won't forget this night.'

They left behind the echoes of their laughter on the lonely road of Delhi.

5

Zamaan, for obvious reasons, was never informed that Falak was staying with Wasim at a place right opposite where Razia was living with her parents. Wasim joined Falak at Razia's place, a night later, for dinner. Razia had prepared baida roti, mutton kebabs and kebab paratha. After finishing dinner, when Falak went back to her place with Wasim, the first thing he did was push her on to the bed. That was his usual drill. A rough fuck after being bailed out. He would have done it the night before had he not gone to sleep early. Deep inside, he hated the fact that his would-be-wife was bailing him out. Wife—a woman. He wasn't conditioned to allow that. Not that anyone else apart from Falak cared about his custody stint, but it hit his ego every time. Falak had mentally prepared herself for the assault. Both the physical as well as the mental.

Wasim stripped her forcefully, getting her naked. Then stripped himself, and he could feel Falak go stiff like she always did. All her muscles would stiffen up the moment Wasim's bare body touched hers. There was no foreplay, no soft kisses, no smiles. Sex between them was a nightmare for Falak. He lifted her legs and thrust his dick inside her without caring whether it ruptured her tissues. As he increased his force, he bit her arm. Like always. Falak knew that if she gave one tiny groan, Wasim would slap her hard, so she kept her mouth shut tight. As his thrusts increased in speed and force, Falak slowly put her plan into action. She wrapped her legs around him. It took Wasim by surprise.

'I love it when you fuck me like this, Wasim,' Falak cried out in a sexy voice. Wasim paused for a trice. He had never heard Falak utter anything except cry during their fuck sessions. He continued with full force again with an arousal that was harder than it was seconds ago. As Wasim was getting to his climax, Falak cupped his ass and pressed her ring on his skin. It was not just an ordinary ring. It was a ring she had purchased after noticing its sharp edge. As Wasim cried out in pleasure, it changed into a long-drawn cry of pain as Falak tore open his skin from his ass to his thighs.

'You bloody bitch!' Wasim thought Falak was trying to kill him.

'Shit, I'm sorry. I forgot I have this ring.' She showed it to Wasim who couldn't argue much on seeing it.

'Just throw it away.' He winced in pain and ran for the first-aid box with blood spurting out of his right ass cheek. Falak remained on the bed with a wicked smile. Then she got up, popped a pill and went to the washroom to see Wasim nursing his wound with a cotton dipped in Dettol.

Suits him. Falak thought. One look at the depth of the wound and she knew he wouldn't be able to flex his glutes for some time now. She went to the kitchen and prepared some haldi milk for Wasim. She brought it to the hall where by then he was sitting on the small sofa on his left bum, careful not to hurt his right bum any further.

'Have this. You'll be all right soon,' Falak said. Wasim didn't argue. He drank up not knowing, like every night, this milk had sleeping pills mixed in. The fact was, even Wasim didn't know Falak was pursuing her MBA. And it was important for her that Wasim slept on time and slept soundly so she could spend the night studying without being noticed.

Once Wasim was snoring, lying on the sofa itself, Falak went to the bedroom and drew out a trunk from under the bed. She opened it, removed all the woollen clothes she had placed on top and took out her MBA books.

She studied till the wee hours of the morning, put the books back in the trunk but this time, she stopped as her eyes fell on an old slam book. It was her college slam book. On an impulse, she picked it up. A smile appeared on her face. She opened the last page of the slam book knowing what it contained. A chapter of her life that she didn't know was over or still continuing in her subconscious mind. She caressed the middle of the last page of the slam book where she had written VEDANT heart FALAK; all in blood. She had never bled for any boy before or after.

In the morning, both Razia and Falak went to the vegetable market together.

'Did it work?' a curious Razia asked. Though she was the other's stepmom, Razia was more childish than Falak. There was an infectious innocence in her that Falak knew had been dampened severely due to the nikah with her father.

'Of course, it had to. My exams are coming. I can't keep getting abused every night and not study.'

'I'm waiting for you to finish your course and get a job. At least one of us would be free.'

'You hate Abbu, isn't it?'

'I don't know. I don't think I know your Abbu much to be able to love or hate him. I only know that right now I'm a prisoner of a situation.'

'We all are.'

'Women, you mean?'

'Women, men, everyone. Like Abbu is a prisoner of his own lust and addiction. To get himself out of his prison, he married you and gifted you a prison. To be free from his prison, you stay here and are helping me do what I want to do.'

They reached the vegetable vendor and started choosing the vegetables they needed.

'I don't think Wasim will leave me that easily. His male ego is sharp to a different level.'

'And I know your mind is wicked to another level. And you will find a way.'

The girls laughed out loud.

'But tell me, did you really have the other guy in mind when Wasim bhai was inside you? Like you told me over the phone?'

Falak glanced at Razia and winked. The latter couldn't stop her laughter. She didn't find it blasphemous because

Falak had told her several times how violent yet poignant her love story had been with Vedant Kaushal. It made her all the more curious both about the man and the story her stepdaughter shared with him.

6

Falak came back home with the veggies. She noticed Wasim had not gone to the university. He was lying down on his stomach resting his ass out. Falak decided to go for a shower before she started preparing the tiffin boxes for the day.

Sitting naked on the bathroom floor, with the tap filling the bucket, Falak's mind was lost. She felt she didn't have much energy left in her. And in moments like these, she only had one escape. Her memories about Vedant. And when she wondered why her love was so violent towards Vedant, she couldn't help but smile nostalgically.

Falak never directly told Vedant that she loved him but she didn't let even one opportunity go by where she didn't make it obvious either. For the first time, she realized she had met a boy who was different from the rest—not because of his actions, looks or what he was—but because she saw him as being different from other boys she had met till that point in time. And that itself was good enough to be named love. To this day she didn't know why she saw him as being different though. And to get his attention, she wrote his name in blood, inspired by a Hindi movie and left the paper on his desk. She thought Vedant would assume, by a divine influence, that it was her blood by only looking at the writing. He didn't. But that didn't deter Falak one bit.

She remembered how she had walked from her home to her college, which was a good 14 km during the monsoon, simply because she couldn't bear to not see Vedant for a day. The roads were flooded in Mumbai from a relentless hour-long downpour in the morning. She didn't have a personal phone at that time, else she would have known that college had been called off. But after coming back from college and nursing her swollen feet, Falak was still smiling. Happy that love made her walk 28 km, she slept with a smile that night telling herself that her love for Vedant had to be true, or else she wouldn't have made the walk.

Then there was a time when she was chosen to represent her college in an inter-college debate competition. But that was also the time when other students, including Vedant, decided amongst themselves that they would go together to Matheran, a hill station near Mumbai. Since the date of the journey and that of the debate collided, Falak dropped the bomb on her professor that she had acquired dengue and then escaped to Matheran, stealing money from her older brother. Of course, nobody in Matheran informed the authorities that she was there and she didn't have dengue, for everyone knew about her love for Vedant. Everyone except Vedant.

As the tap filled the bucket and started overflowing, the water came in touch with her bare feet. The coldness of it brought Falak back to awareness. She had a stupid smile on her face thinking of her silly and mad behaviour. As she stood up, she wondered if she should have not done any of those things and instead should have simply told Vedant that she loved him. Innocence perhaps makes one forgo the obvious and pursue the most unobvious thing with passion.

Falak closed the tap and had her bath. Even while bathing, though, her thoughts were about certain what-ifs. In all these years she had indulged in such what-ifs a countless number of times. What if she had actually told Vedant her feelings directly and he accepted them? Would they have been in a relationship now? Humans can find an excuse to fall in love as much as they can find a reason to fall out of love as well. Would their relationship have lasted? Vedant wouldn't have beaten her for sure or raped her in the name of sex. That wasn't him. And that's why he was attractive at a core level.

As she was drying herself, Falak wondered if everything good, with the touch of a human, becomes stale. Did love live by this paradox as well? She quickly dressed up for college and called Razia.

'Do you think if Vedant and I would have been in a domestic set-up, we would have also become an emotional zero?'

'Are you trying to find the answer to it after already having an answer that would validate the fact that it's good you guys didn't make it?' Razia shot back. This was precisely why, amongst a whole lot of other reasons, Falak loved her.

'What if I say yes?'

'All I know is to get married is way easier than to remain married. And by remaining married I'm not saying just sharing a bedroom.'

'So you are saying one should become a parent to the proximity the couple shares after marriage or maybe living in?' Falak reached Wasim's bike and stood there reclining on it.

'Proximity parenting. That's a nice one. That's what I was hinting at. We all love to love but we fail to parent our love. Love's a baby. And if we don't parent it well, it can grow up to be a difficult or a bad child.'

'And that's where most relationships become an emotional zero, I guess. Makes sense. But since I loved Vedant so much, I think I would have definitely been a good proximity parent.'

'And him?'

'I don't want to think about that. Some things should remain a fantasy.'

'Indeed.'

'But I do wish to meet him once.'

'Why?'

Falak got on her bike, started it and then said, 'I don't know. I'll figure it out when I meet him. But I really want to meet him.'

'Inshallah,' Razia said.

'You know, something had happened during the college farewell.'

'What? You guys did it?' Razia sounded excited.

'No. I remember this so distinctly. Everyone was at the farewell party. I'd excused myself to go to the washroom. When I moved out and was on my way to rejoin the party, I was stopped by Vedant.'

There was a pause. Falak was momentarily lost. Razia grew impatient.

'Go on. Don't create *sasta* suspense!'

'He came up to me. Looked deep into my eyes. I could feel my knees trembling. And trust me, I was really expecting he was going to say yes to my proposal, finally. The more time he took to speak, the more I was preparing my reaction in my head. But what he said didn't make sense then. Doesn't make sense now when I think back.'

'What the hell did he say?'

'That he was sorry. That's it. I-am-sorry. Those were his words.'

'Didn't you ask him why he said it?'

'I was about to and I think he would have clarified it as well if a couple of friends hadn't intervened and pulled him away to the party. I too went back. Our eyes kept looking for each other but we never talked after that. Neither that night nor till now.'

'What was he sorry for?'

'I don't know. And that's also why I want to meet him and ask. Was he sorry that he wanted to say yes to my proposal but for some reason, he couldn't? Or was he there trying to sympathize with me, knowing my feelings for him? Or . . . what was it?'

There was momentary silence after which Falak spoke up, 'Anyway, Razia sweety. Time for my tiffin clients now. Talk to you later,' and she ended the call.

Falak drove on, away from thoughts of Vedant and preparing for her everyday battle once again.

7

Falak was tired of living on a tightrope. Whatever she earned from her tiffin service went into her house rent, electricity bill, petrol for the bike and groceries as fixed costs, including the things she had to buy for her tiffin service. The money for the books she had to buy was given to her by Razia.

'Shut up!' Razia had scolded her when Falak said she couldn't take her money. 'I'm your mother.' There was a momentary eye-lock between them. Then the two girls burst into laughter. Seconds later, Falak's eyes were moist.

'You know, Razia, you have come as *sukoon*, peace, in my life,' Falak said. 'I never had such support from my own parents. I think the only thing Abbu did right was to marry you. But then, I know he shouldn't have.'

'And you have come into my life as *umeed*, hope. I don't think I would have been able to live half of what I have with you if I was in Mumbai with your Abbu.'

'That's true.'

It was Razia who had a talk with the elder brother of one of her neighbours who worked in a bank for Falak's education loan to complete her MBA. For the repayment, the EMIs would begin from the month she took up a job after her MBA.

Falak parked the bike, wiped the sweat oozing out of her hijab and then took the stairs up to her flat. She couldn't wait to take a shower. Delhi's summer was at its peak. She unlocked the door. Nobody was inside. It surprised her as Wasim was injured. Usually, Wasim used to leave in the morning, for god knows where, and come back late. As Falak put her footwear by the main door, she heard a song playing in the bedroom. So Wasim was home. She went to the bedroom and saw Wasim's phone was on the bed. From it, a sexy Hindi song was playing. Falak picked up the phone. It was an Instagram reel of a girl who was showing off her thick thighs. A quick glance told her the name of the account was Naagin Ki Naani. Falak was pissed off. As Wasim came out of the bathroom with wet hands, trousers low and the drawstring untied, she immediately knew why exactly he was inside. He was masturbating to Naagin Ki Naani and had gone to wash up. Falak hurled the phone at him.

'Have you gone mad? Do you know what's the price of the phone? More than your fucking worth,' Wasim bellowed, picking up the phone. There was a crack on the screen guard, but the rest seemed fine.

'Do I know? Of course I do because I'm paying the EMIs of that fucking phone. And my worth was decided the day I chose you. Aren't you ashamed, Wasim? I'm working my ass off, trying to get everything sorted and here you are, sitting and masturbating to some whore all day.'

'Falak, our women don't say foul stuff.'

'Really? I'm sorry. I won't say anything. I'd rather shove your face inside a dog's ass. Come.' Falak charged at Wasim.

The latter, by now, knew about his sheer incapability of pacifying Falak when her beast mode was on. Wasim managed to sneak out of the bedroom though Falak had caught his tee by then. He jerked her hand off him, rushed to the main door and ran out from there. Falak sat down, frustrated. What had she done to deserve such daily harassment? Leaving Wasim was also not an option since, being the asshole that he was, the first thing he would do was call Zamaan and tell him what his daughter and wife were up to. It was a leverage because of which she took a lot of shit from him, like a sitting duck. But it was time to give Wasim a taste of his own medicine.

Wasim came out of the masjid after reading his namaaz in the evening. He took out his phone, which was on silent mode, and saw there were five missed calls from Falak. He called her back. The woman who spoke seemed like she had forgotten what had happened in the morning.

'Hey baby, it's been a long time since you called your friends home. I'm preparing galouti kebabs and parathas. If you want, you can bring your friends home.'

For a trice, Wasim thought he hadn't heard her right.

'Are you sure?'

'Absolutely, jaan,' Falak said and ended the call. Wasim's friends were like him. There were four of them and all were studying in JNU for the past eight years. They simply worked for the political party that gave them the money and to-do list. It was because of this backing that none of them stayed in custody for long.

It was 8 p.m. when Wasim came home with his friends. He was still wearing the tee and trousers that he had on while rushing out of the house in the morning. As the five of them settled down, Falak saw they had brought bottles of Coke with them. She let them converse for some time, during which she too came in and greeted them. Then, when everybody said they were hungry, Falak went to the kitchen and warmed the kebabs and parathas.

'What an aroma!' remarked one of Wasim's friends.

'You're really lucky, Wasim bhai,' said another. 'Mine doesn't even know the difference between salt and sugar. Idiot, she is,' he added.

'But you said she knows how to suck,' a third blurted out. The men burst into vulgar laughter.

'That's exactly why I've still kept her as my girlfriend.'

Falak was listening hard to all they were discussing. To belittle their woman in whatever form they could was their favourite sport. Falak put out five plates and then loaded them with her mouth-watering kebabs. She put the parathas in a hot case. Then she took the plates and hot case outside.

They didn't have a dining table. The boys were sitting on the floor on a mat.

'Put some newspapers down,' Falak had said before bringing in the food. Wasim had spread out a couple of old newspapers so the food could be put on them.

Falak served the food and left. She wasn't supposed to eat with them or even stay for more time than required. She went to the bedroom and locked it from inside. Though it was hot, she didn't switch the fan on. Then she lay down on the bed with her phone, opened a Johnny Sins porn video and started watching it at full volume. She knew well that, with the fan off, the sound would invariably go to the hall room.

As the moaning and grunting started in the video, Falak smiled, realizing the boys had gone all quiet. There were no jokes being cracked, no loud laughter or even talk. Pin-drop silence amidst which Johnny Sins and his girl were giving each other pleasure. There was a knock on the bedroom door. Falak was more than ready for it.

'Open the door, Falak.' It was Wasim. From his tone, she knew he felt humiliated. Falak didn't budge for some time and kept playing the video. The moment came when Wasim kicked the door. That's when Falak paused the video, got up and opened the door. Wasim entered and locked the door.

'What are you doing?'

'Watching what you were watching. Why, what happened?'

'You know my friends will think you are a whore?'

Falak smirked and said, 'Please tell me you think of me otherwise? If you did, you would have been a different person.' Falak just finished her sentence when she felt Wasim's hard hand on her face. For the next half hour, he kept beating her. Punches, kicks, slaps. She too hit him back but Wasim was physically stronger than her. He even pulled her by the hair and slammed her against the wall. After half an hour, when Falak was on the floor, not moving, he opened the door. His friends had gone. The food was left the way it was when he had come into the bedroom. Wasim sat down and started weeping. Not because he had beaten her but because he knew the other friends would laugh at him behind his back.

Inside, Falak smiled through her injuries. She had won in her attempt to ridicule him and make him feel what she felt every day with him. Her cheeks hurt and her body was aching but she focused on the happiness Wasim's weeping triggered in her.

Wasim didn't come back home that night. He left after some time, weeping like a baby. He didn't know how he would face his friends again. Falak crawled to her phone in the room and ordered some first-aid using a delivery app. The medicines came within ten minutes.

'You need any help?' the delivery boy asked, seeing Falak's facial bruises. She tried but couldn't talk. So she simply shook her head, no. And closed the door. As Falak gathered all her energy to go to the washroom, she wasn't surprised to see her reflection. Her face was more battered than normal but what she was proud of was that it had not had any effect whatsoever on her soul. Falak took some cotton out from the freshly delivered medicines, dipped it in Dettol and started wiping all the areas where she was injured. She promised herself she wouldn't cry for she knew this would have happened, but her victory was that she had injured Wasim exactly where she had intended to. His 'chivalrous' yet brittle male ego. Not that things would change from here on, but she had lived enough taking the punches. Now for every punch, she would kick back. Result or no result. Consequences or no consequences.

As Falak felt pain every time she dabbed the soft cotton dipped in Dettol on her wounds, someone's words ricocheted in her mind. Perhaps the only male she had ever respected in her life.

'You're one of the strongest females I have ever seen in my life, Falak. Whoever marries you will be really lucky,' Vedant had once told her when they were in college. She was finishing her BCom while he was finishing his Mass Com.

Someone was right about her.

8

Razia rushed to Falak's flat the moment she saw her facial condition on the video call.

'Can't we just kill Wasim and not get caught?' Razia asked. She was simmering with anger.

'How many Wasims will we kill?' Falak asked. 'It's not a man we need to kill, it's a thought. It's a schooling. It's gender insensitivity. It's gender supremacy. And a hell of a lot of other shit.'

Razia knew Falak was right. The situation they and girls like them were in wasn't the trap. Their birth into it was the trap. They could run away for some time from such things but eventually, they would have to suffer it. It wasn't about religion either. Girls from other religions also suffered. It was the deep-seated, sick-to-the-stomach patriarchal mindset that was beyond religion. And logic too. Razia made some paya soup for Falak and continued talking while helping her sip it.

'You'll stay with me now,' Razia said.

'I wish that was the solution. I can slap Wasim but if I ignore him, he will go to Abbu.'

Razia knew Falak was right. If Wasim went to Zamaan, chances were both Falak and Razia would be called to Mumbai.

'Then don't do things that turn the beast in him on,' Razia said.

'That depends on Wasim. If he doesn't do things that turn on the monster in me, then I won't do anything to bring out the beast in him.'

Razia thought for some time while helping Falak have the soup.

'You shouldn't have left him,' Razia said. Falak gave her a sharp glance. She knew whom Razia meant by 'him'. Not Wasim.

'I didn't leave him. I never had him as such. Vedant and I were friends. I don't know why but I've never seen so much respect in any man's eyes as he had for me. Maybe because he knew where I was coming from and yet was trying to break through. Maybe he was in awe of my stubbornness. I thought it was love from his side but—'

'Wasn't it from your side?'

'Totally, it was. I have never loved a man more than Vedant. I had told him that as well but he never gave me a clear answer. Neither a clear yes nor a clear no.'

'Why? Did he have a girlfriend?'

'No. Not that I knew of. Vedant was different. Some of our common friends, who knew I had the hots for him, told me that he was focused on his career and believed that relationships bogged one down. Vedant was a detached guy.'

'It wasn't a religious thing, right? Like you are a Muslim and he's a Hindu?'

'I don't think so. He never gave me those Islamophobic vibes at all. On the contrary, he never looked at me and my hijab the way other guys and girls did at times. It was like he was comfortable with our different beliefs.'

'Hmm.' The soup bowl was empty now. Razia gave Falak a tissue and went to the kitchen to place the bowl in the sink.

'I've told my maid to do your housework too. You don't have to give her any money. I'll take care of it.' Razia came back to Falak. 'Where is he now?'

'Where else? Must be sniffing around like a dog at the university.'

Razia shook her head and said, 'I meant Vedant. Where is he?'

'Allah knows. All I know is he isn't active on social media, his old number isn't working—the one he used in college—and none of our common friends knows where he is.'

'That's strange.'

'Good in a way. If he was available, the itch in me would have made me get in touch.'

'You want to?'

'Why not? Maybe he isn't the detached type any more. Maybe he regrets he didn't say yes to me.'

'Did you propose to him? Like a legit proposal?'

'Yes. With flowers, chocolates and a card. I had saved the money from my salary as a tuition teacher to kids during that time,' Falak said and shifted on the bed a little, looking at the wardrobe.

'Just open the wardrobe. There is a key inside where I keep my bras.'

Razia did as she was told. She found the key.

'Open the lowest drawer.'

Razia did. And saw a card. She picked it up and turned with excitement.

'Don't tell me this is that . . .'

Falak nodded and blushed. Razia brought the card to the bed, opened it and started reading from it:

'My first love, Vedant. I guess those first few words told you what I intend to write further. Yes, I love you. Don't know from when. But I know I'll love you forever. Here's hoping you say yes and make a girl happy.'

'Gosh! What fucking stupidity. Just look at my language. Who writes like that?' Falak genuinely looked embarrassed.

'Grown-ups always define innocence as stupidity,' Razia said.

'Anyway, he had given the card back to me. So, it was a no.'

A few silent seconds later, Falak spoke as if she was talking to herself, 'That moment was so important in my life back then. Now I don't even know if I should be happy or sad about the fact that Vedant never happened to me the way I wanted.'

Neither said anything.

Razia went away after keeping all the necessary things beside Falak. The latter messaged her clients that she was sick and wouldn't be able to give them tiffin for two days. For the next two days, Falak mostly stayed in bed. She saw Wasim come in but not speak a word. Typical of him after an abusive bout. Razia used to come during the day. The painkillers had her sleeping most of the day. Two days turned into five. From the sixth day onwards, it was back to monotony. Prepare tiffin for her clients, study, attend college, finish assignments. Except Wasim kept away, much to her relief. And whenever she lay in bed, with her eyes on the ceiling, she kept wondering what would have happened if Vedant had said yes to her proposal. Would her life have changed? Altered for the better? Suddenly, Falak felt she was going through an existential crisis. Vedant wasn't any knight in shining armour. And had he said yes, there would have been turbulence since their religious beliefs were different. But that turbulence would have stemmed from people's frustratingly limited respect for others. Would it have created a problem for the two of them? Falak had never met Vedant's parents. But she knew her father. Falak shook her head realizing that what-if was a waste of time. Her reality was Wasim. Her reality was she was injured. And her reality was she had to study, secure a degree and free herself from everybody who wanted to cage her.

Ten more days went by. Wasim didn't talk to her. Nor did Falak initiate any conversation. She used to leave food at home before going to college and came back to find it had been eaten. In a way, Falak felt comfortable in the non-communicative dynamics that had set in. She even hoped it stayed this way till her semester exams, which were around the corner, were over. She would be able to study in peace. One night before the semester exam, though, Wasim barged into the bedroom. Till then, he had been sleeping on the hall room sofa. Before Falak could figure out what was he up to, he picked her up from the study table and threw her on the bed. And didn't leave till he came inside her. It was nothing new for Falak. She intentionally didn't budge much for she didn't want more injuries before her exam. Once Wasim left the room, she got up, washed herself and then came back to study.

The exams went well. Two more semesters were left before Falak could pass with her master's and secure a job. Fifteen days later, however, she missed her menses. A scared Falak rushed to the nearby chemist and bought a pregnancy kit. She came back home and went straight to the washroom. As she waited for the test to bear results, Falak realized those seconds were the most tense of her life. She could neither think nor remain blank. The worst ideas were coming to her mind. She couldn't afford to be pregnant at that point in time. She had her whole career on the line. And if Wasim even had an inkling, he would inform Zamaan and a nikah would be executed immediately. Which would seal her life's ambitions forever. She kept praying to the Almighty under her breath that her fears wouldn't turn real. But a few seconds later, she knew her prayers hadn't been heard.

Falak Sultana was pregnant.

9

Falak waited till Wasim went out. Then she broke down, sitting alone in her hall room. For most women, it was great news. That there was a life blossoming within her. It somewhere validated her divine right to be a mother. Not for Falak. She saw the news as a major roadblock to all her dreams. Rightly so. She messaged Razia to come home immediately. The latter called the moment she read her message, sensing something must be very wrong. When Falak didn't answer her call, Razia knew it was something worse.

It took Razia ten minutes to come to Falak's doorstep. She found the main door open. She entered with her heart in her mouth. Seeing Falak on the sofa, she breathed normally. Razia closed the door behind her and came to Falak, who was sitting like a zombie staring at the ceiling. She could see dry tears at the corners of her eyes.

'Will you tell me what happened?'

'I'm pregnant,' Falak said, without any emotion. There was silence.

'Didn't you have the pill?' Razia asked. Her voice gave away the fact that it was blasphemous for Falak not to use it.

'Just this time, I didn't. I actually forgot to. I had my studies and . . .' Falak's voice trailed away. She hadn't looked this defeated even when she had been beaten up by Wasim. Razia couldn't bear to see her like that. And she knew pretty well it wasn't the fact that she was pregnant that had bogged her down.

'Don't worry. We'll figure out a way,' Razia said, trying to pep her up.

'To?'

'To abort this,' Razia said. And then added, 'Don't tell me you want to keep it?'

Falak just needed someone to voice her own thoughts.

'No, I can't afford to keep it. I can't have a child who is a product of domestic violence. If it was out of love, I would have still . . .'

'Philosophy later,' Razia shut her down. And sat down thinking. Falak didn't disturb her. Minutes later, she saw Razia calling someone.

'Salaam, Furkan miya. How are you?'

Falak could guess what the other person was saying from Razia's response.

'I'm good too. I know I'm calling all of a sudden but this is for someone close to me,' Razia said and waited for the response. She replied, 'Sure. I'll be there.'

Razia ended the call and saw Falak's expectant face.

'That was Furkan. The one I would have married if your Abbu hadn't arrived on the scene,' Razia said the whole thing with a sigh. She came to sit by Falak.

'You never told me this,' Falak said with a tinge of complaint in her voice.

'Furkan and I had met at a cousin's wedding in Hyderabad. He hails from there. A brilliant guy. He is a gynaecologist. But still growing as a doctor. He came from a humble background but used his sharp mind wisely to become a doctor. Very learned. Very informed. Very helpful. Very . . .'

'Much in love with you?' Falak completed. Razia remained quiet. That was not only an affirmation but also a confession that she too was in love with Furkan.

'I guess so,' Razia said.

'May I see a picture?' Falak asked. For the first time that morning, Falak was focusing on something other than her pregnancy. Razia immediately opened her phone with eagerness, which was a sure giveaway. She looked up at Falak and knew she was caught.

'You guess so, huh? I knew it from your silence only,' Falak said. She looked at Furkan's picture. He did look like a studious and intelligent guy. Though Falak didn't say it aloud, she felt bad for Razia for having to settle for her uneducated, loathsome Abbu, leaving behind someone as polished and gentle as Furkan.

'Let's meet him tomorrow,' Razia said.

'But you said he was in Hyderabad.'

'Yeah. He was studying back then. Now he has opened a small clinic here in Delhi,' Razia said and started scrolling through her phone.

'He shifted for you, na?'

Razia didn't reply. She pretended she hadn't heard Falak. The latter repeated herself and then saw tears oozing out of Razia's eyes. Falak reached out to her only to realize her body was shivering.

'I will never forget what you told me about Vedant,' Razia spoke slowly. Falak's curious eyes made her continue. 'That sometimes some people are not in your destiny. Period. Doesn't matter how much you long for them. Furkan is that person for me. We came into each other's life but we aren't destined for the other.'

The girls didn't talk to each other for some time. The silence between them was triggering a lot of self-conversation, which they solemnly engaged in.

The next day, Falak accompanied Razia to Dr Furkan. The clinic was a tiny one. Just enough space for four or five patients to wait while one assistant took down their names. There was another small, closed cabin for the doctor to sit and examine his patients. Razia could have taken priority over the four people waiting before her but she didn't. They entered the cabin only when their names were called out by the assistant.

Razia was the first one to enter the cabin. Furkan stood up on seeing her. Did he do so for all his patients? She wondered but knew she would never know.

'Salaam,' Furkan said. He never averted his eyes from Razia. It was as if Falak didn't exist in the room. The latter understood but didn't mind. This was a glimpse of gold dust in their otherwise iron-rust life.

'Walekum assalam,' Razia said, feeling her throat going dry. Many a time she had wondered if she would ever meet

Furkan again, especially after her marriage, but never did she imagine it would be in his clinic, and for the reason that brought her here. Razia remembered having a phone call with Furkan when he shifted to Delhi. This was three days before her marriage.

'Did you shift because I'm here? I won't be here for long.' Then she had to tell him those painful words: 'My nikah is in three days.'

There was a pause.

'I know,' Furkan said. 'I came here as I thought I could breathe the same air as you.'

As a kid, Razia used to read words like these in pulpy romance novels, fantasizing that someday someone would use them for her. But as she grew up, she realized the books themselves were fantasy. Nothing that was written in them happened for real. In fact, the books were written for people to use as a soft cushion against the reality they were living.

'Please sit down.' Furkan pushed forward his chair as there were only two in the room.

'I'm all right. This is my daughter, Falak.'

Furkan wasn't surprised seeing such a grown-up, almost-her-age daughter. He wasn't sure if Razia knew it but from the time she had told Furkan about her nikah, he had searched for all the information about whom she was getting married to. And as he got it, he understood that no girl, especially one like Razia, would marry a person like Zamaan unless she was indebted to him in some way. It was a deal-marriage.

Razia gestured to Falak to sit. She did.

'She found out she is pregnant. And we want an abortion,' Razia said. She figured it was better to get to the point than be lost in the past.

'When did you have your last menses?' Furkan asked Falak. She told him an approximate date as she didn't remember exactly. Furkan took his notepad and scribbled a blood test. A beta HCG test.

'Just do this test. You can get it done from the diagnostic centre nearby.'

'This test is for?'

'I'm sure you must have used some kit to determine the pregnancy.'

Falak nodded.

'Sometimes kits are faulty too. We need to be absolutely sure. The result of this blood test will help us to be sure,' Furkan said.

'Okay.'

'And please show me the report,' he looked at Razia and said.

'May we WhatsApp it to you?' Razia asked. The first thought Furkan had on hearing it was that the ladies perhaps weren't in a position to visit him regularly. He had already understood the pregnancy hadn't happened in a desirable situation. He didn't want to ask further questions and risk embarrassing the ladies. But as he looked into Razia's eyes, he understood there was another dimension to the mention of WhatsApp.

'Sure, you can WhatsApp me the report. Not a problem.'

'Shukriya,' Razia said and asked, 'Your fees?'

'You don't have to . . .'

'Please, I insist,' Razia said.

'You can give it to Abida outside.'

'Thank you so much,' Razia smiled and both left the room.

Leaving the clinic, the girls first went to the nearby diagnostic centre Furkan had told them about. Falak gave a blood sample. They asked if the reports could be emailed, which was allowed. Then the girls took an auto to the nearest metro station. As Falak and Razia were returning home, Falak couldn't stop talking.

'Furkan is a real gentleman. I think I'll have a crush on him at some point in time. I like men like him. Educated. Gentle. Respectful.'

Razia blushed and said, 'So do I.'

'Such a kinky thing. Mother and stepdaughter eyeing the same man.'

'Shut up! I'm not eyeing him.'

'Then what was the WhatsApp mention for?' Falak was in no mood to let Razia off.

'Damn, was it that obvious?'

'Like hell it was. You wanted to tell him you were available for chatting.'

'I hope he got the clue.'

'Even if he didn't, at least now another person is waiting for the blood test report as desperately as me,' Falak laughed. Razia hushed her. Then looked at her face bordered by the hijab she was wearing.

'The best thing I like about you, Falak,' she said, caressing her forehead, 'is that you smile through your tough times.' She looked around and added, 'Nobody in this metro would be able to guess you are carrying a life in your womb and tension in your mind.'

'What to do, Razia sweety, if people like us don't know how to smile through tough times, we won't ever be able to smile,' Falak said. Razia did sense a bit of an emotional choke-up by the time she ended the statement, but she chose to focus on her stepdaughter's smile. They reached home. Razia asked Falak to rest while she went home to see what her father was up to. He needed support all the time. This was one reason why her life had changed completely.

Around evening, when Razia was preparing tea for herself, the doorbell rang. Razia opened the door, casually. And stood there hoping the sudden surge in her heartbeats wasn't felt by the man standing at the door. It was Zamaan. And he had come to Delhi with no intimation. He pushed her aside and stepped into the house. He sat on a sofa, wiping his sweat with his hand.

'*Behenchod*. Such a whore-ish summer this is.'

'Give me some water,' Zamaan said, looking around. 'Where's that fool? Falak?' he added.

According to the story they had told Zamaan, Falak used to stay with Razia.

10

'She has gone to the market,' Razia said.

'Good. It's good she is staying with you and learning what women are born to do,' Zamaan said.

Razia came to him with a towel and said, 'Why don't you take a shower? You will feel better.'

Zamaan smiled at Razia. She may have been just twenty-four but she had all the qualities of a good wife, be it off or on the bed. The thought of ravaging Razia later that night was already giving Zamaan a stir in his balls. He took the towel, opened his bag, took out some fresh clothes and went to the washroom. Razia immediately called Falak.

'Your Abbu is here unannounced.'

'Ya Allah! This was the last thing I needed,' Falak shot back. Their contingency plan was on. Falak went to the small suitcase that was kept forever packed in case Abbu arrived unannounced. She picked it up, called Wasim and told him Zamaan was there. Only in this regard were Wasim and Falak on the same team for their own selfish reasons. Wasim was not supposed to call or visit her while Zamaan was there. And he respected that rule for his own good. For if Zamaan knew Wasim was living-in with his daughter, he would not only kill

Falak but him too. Thus, even if there was always a danger of Wasim ratting out to Zamaan about her MBA and tiffin business, Falak also knew he wouldn't go unscathed either.

By the time Zamaan came out of the shower, Falak had arrived with her suitcase while Razia had quickly bought some veggies lest Zamaan be suspicious.

'You look like shit. What are you up to?' Zamaan said, on seeing Falak.

'Nothing, Abbu. I only stay at home and help Ammi.'

'Fool,' Zamaan muttered under his breath like he had been doing since he had seen her for the first time in the clinic where she was born. Zamaan was the perfect stereotype for a man who was conditioned to see a woman as a child-bearing machine at her core with ancillary responsibilities like looking after the house, looking after her man and expertly taming her desires, which shouldn't pop their ugly heads up any time in life.

After having a sumptuous meal prepared by Razia who was helped by Falak, Zamaan slept, snoring away shamelessly. He didn't care to even ask how Razia's father was doing. In the kitchen, the girls were having an anxious conversation.

'How many days is he here for?' Falak asked.

'No idea!' Razia said.

'Thank God he came after my exams. I can still alternate my college but my tiffin service? I can't lose the clients.'

Razia could understand the pain in her voice. The one thing Falak had not mentioned was her pregnancy.

'Did the report come?'

'Yes. Half an hour back. The test is positive.'

'WhatsApp me the report. I'll send it to Furkan.'

Falak immediately did that. That night, after Zamaan had his way sexually with Razia and went off to sleep, she WhatsApp-ed the report to Furkan and messaged Falak as well. The latter was in the other room. Furkan messaged her saying they should meet the next day. Razia didn't promise Furkan they would be there. Instead, she messaged Falak for suggestions.

Do I have to get admitted to any clinic? Falak's message read.

I suppose so. Wait, let me ask him. Razia messaged and after two minutes, messaged again: *Yes, you'll have to. But he said it would all be done in a day.*

Normally it wouldn't have been a problem but what do we do with Abbu here?

I've something in mind.

What?

Falak couldn't believe what Razia messaged her but she knew that if Razia said it, she would execute it.

The next day, Razia threw up and then told Zamaan she wasn't feeling well. And needed to visit a doctor. As Zamaan went out with Razia to the doctor, Falak rushed to Furkan's clinic. She was admitted to a nearby clinic which was bigger and where Furkan was associated as well. It took a total of eight hours for the medical abortion to take place.

'You need to have bed rest,' Furkan told Falak.

'I will. And don't message Razia now. Abbu is here. Once he leaves, she will message you. Not because she wants an affair but I think she misses your friendship.'

Furkan heard her with patience. Then he said, 'I understand. I am in love with her and won't do anything that would tarnish her image.'

Hearing a man say that was a refreshing change. Falak thanked him once again and left. When she reached home, she did have a little pain in her abdomen but what was bothering her more was what Razia was up to. She did call and message her but there was no reply. She thought of calling Zamaan but according to the plan, Razia would keep Zamaan busy with her projected bad health and tell him that Falak had gone to one of her cousins in Noida to deliver a gift since the cousin had delivered a baby recently.

It was Zamaan who opened the door.

'You gave the gift?' he asked.

'Yes. Where's Ammi?'

'Why? Don't pretend as if she is your real mother. She is a bitch, understand that from today.'

With that, Falak knew something bad must have happened. As she went inside, her jaws clenched on seeing Razia's swollen face and an eye that looked busted. Razia's father was lying down in the same room. He had emptied his usual spot in the hall room for Zamaan. Falak ignored him as she went near Razia, who somehow managed to talk lying down.

'All good?' she asked.

Falak nodded.

'What happened?'

Razia took her time to speak. When she did, she spoke softly.

'We came back from the doctor. Your Abbu wanted to get physical but I'd got my periods this morning so I was in pain. I asked him if we could do it a couple of days later. He got angry thinking I was denying him what was his. And then . . .'

And then . . . Falak knew the rest. Her jaws locked with anger as she noticed a couple of teardrops oozing out from Razia's eyes.

She didn't say much. Falak retired to her room and didn't move till Zamaan bellowed from the hall room,

'Will we be not having dinner tonight, that too with two ladies in the house?'

By then Falak had decided. Things couldn't go on like this. Both Razia and she deserved anything but this. What she had decided would have consequences and collateral damage but it was sheer anger that didn't make her think of any other option or even give rationality a chance. And it wasn't anger that had brewed just during that one evening. It was an anger that had grown in her heart and taken deep root in her soul. It was an anger that could no longer be negated without strong action. It was an anger that pushed one off the edge.

Falak got down from her bed and went to the kitchen. She prepared the dough for the parathas she was making for Zamaan and Wasim as well. The latter had messaged her saying if she didn't give him food, he would talk to Zamaan. It fanned her anger further. She served the parathas with some mutton kheema that was there in the fridge. With the excuse of getting some veggies for the next day, Falak went to her flat and gave Wasim the food. She came back and prepared some paya soup for Razia. Zamaan was done with his dinner by then.

When Falak came out of Razia's room, after helping her have the soup, she saw Zamaan dead on the floor near the bathroom. She imagined Wasim too must be dead in his flat for she had mixed an entire bottle of rat poison in the dough with which she'd prepared their parathas. She cleaned the froth coming out of Zamaan's mouth. Then went to her room, wrote a note, packed her bag like a girl on a mission and left the house. She went to her flat where she did the same clean-up with Wasim's dead body. Then she stuffed her bag with some more of her belongings, booked an Uber auto to Nizamuddin Railway Station and left the flat.

It was only an hour later that Razia came out of her room since Falak wasn't responding to her verbal calls. Seeing Zamaan on the floor, she sensed what Falak had pulled off. A little examination told her Zamaan was dead. Realizing this, Razia tried to but didn't feel any remorse. She read the note that was kept beside Zamaan's dead body.

Abbu won't disturb you any more. Wasim won't disturb me either. Cook up whatever story you want to. I know you're good at it. Your father can be a good alibi for you. Be happy with Furkan. Don't worry about me. I shall be back but not any time soon. Love you like I've never loved anyone. Destroy this after reading. Heal soon, Razia sweety.

It was signed 'Falak'. Through the bruises, swelling and injuries on her face, Razia did try to smile. And it came naturally. Just like Falak and her fight against life had happened.

[illegible]

When light came [illegible] hours after [illegible] dead [illegible]

[illegible] the same [illegible]

[illegible]

[illegible]

[illegible]

BOOK 3: THE GIRLS MEET THE BOY

1

'Falak Sultana,' the driver said, reading from his phone. The name sounded like that of a hippie to Nityami. Anyway, she couldn't care less. Nityami put on her AirPods, went to her playlist and closed her eyes. The songs were all romantic ones. From the time she got to know there was a chance to find Vedant by the Gurudongmar Lake, her daydreaming had gone to the next level. She kept playing her favourite songs and dreaming about their meeting after all these years. She used to listen to certain songs when in school. Every time she closed her eyes, she would see Vedant then. Now too, those songs were bringing back Vedant's face. But it was the Vedant she knew. A face without a trace of moustache, clean supple skin, a protruding Adam's apple, messy hair, taller than average, lean, exuding boyish charm and with a birthmark on his right arm. *What did he look like now?* she wondered. The Facebook display picture, which also seemed to be from college times, wasn't a clear one either. Perhaps taken from a low-pixel camera of yore. As the songs took over, a stupid smile spread and stayed on her face in response to the daydream that had been switched on in her mind.

Nityami woke up hearing some hushed talk. Realizing she had dozed off, she opened her eyes wide and said aloud, 'Where am I?' It was a little too loud and sudden for the other two in the car. The girl sitting beside her—Falak—glanced at her. She was the one who was talking on her phone in a hushed tone. The driver turned back in a trice to see if all was okay and then focused on his driving.

'You're in a car. Going most probably to Gangtok. What did you think?' Falak asked. She ended the call with Razia.

'I know I'm going to Gangtok but I just dozed off.'

'Yeah, I know you dozed off.'

Nityami quickly took out her phone and checked her destination on the GPS. It was still showing three hours to her hotel in Gangtok, Hotel High Top. She was supposed to spend the night there, then take a cab to the lake the next day. It meant she had slept for two hours, as the time to reach Hotel High Top from Bagdogra Airport was five hours. Nityami turned to glance at Falak. She was registering her presence for the first time.

She has a style statement, Nityami thought, looking at Falak's dhoti-pajamas, oversized shirt, lots of colourful beads on her hands and a hijab whose colour was in perfect contrast to her shirt.

'Anything wrong?' Falak suddenly glanced at Nityami, who wasn't ready for her.

'What? No.'

'You're checking me out, so I thought.'

'I'm sorry. I was just . . .' Nityami swallowed a lump in her throat and continued, '. . . looking around.'

'Oh okay. I'm sorry then.' Falak said with a smile. It was then that Nityami noticed faint injury marks on her face.

The driver's phone buzzed with a notification. Being a weird sound, it made the girls glance up at him. He took up the phone with one hand and checked the notification. As he opened the Instagram app from where the notification had come, another car came speeding up, making him drop the phone on the adjacent seat and quickly manoeuvre the car to safety. As the phone landed on the seat, it opened to the last reel the driver had watched. And the BG music took over the silence in the cab. Falak leaned a little forward to look at the reel. The driver by then had the car under control. He picked up his phone.

'What reel was that?' Falak asked, curiously. As if what she had seen wasn't something new.

The driver looked at her via the rear-view mirror and said, blushing, 'It's a girl's reel.'

'That I understood but may I know the username? I think I've seen her,' Falak said. Nityami, not caring about either the reel or the driver or even what Falak was saying, opened her bottle of water.

'It's Naagin Ki Naani's reel.'

Nityami spewed out the water from her mouth straight in front of her on hearing the name.

'She is a phenomenon!' the driver said.

'Are you all right?' Falak asked.

'I'm sorry, yes I am,' said an embarrassed Nityami. She took a few tissues out of her bag and wiped the seat. The driver did not seem to be bothered.

'I know she is famous. Even my boyfriend is a fan. And now I remember where I had seen her. On his phone,' Falak said, looking at the driver in the mirror.

The driver smiled and said, 'You have a naughty boyfriend then.'

Falak knew why he said it. But Nityami couldn't glance at the driver. Of all people, she wasn't expecting him to be a follower. She had created the ID with a lot of anger and where it had reached today was nothing short of a comic miracle. She had 500K followers. She had unfollowed everyone so her profile showed: 15 posts. 500K followers. 0 Following. The 0 following part gave her immense pride. And satisfied her ego. She felt important. And that important self of hers, right then, did not have any excuse to not feel naked. Not only the driver, the girl next to her said that even her boyfriend was a fan. This was her first fan moment where someone who wasn't on her radar had identified her profile right in front of her.

I wish I could tell them I was Naagin Ki Naani, Nityami thought and switching on her selfie camera, looked at herself. A small semblance of a pimple on her chin which had turned the area red, baby fat well embedded on her face, short-flat nose and . . . Nityami shut off the camera. There was nothing exceptional about her face. She knew it. What was the need to check and further demoralize oneself? On the whole, she may have not been a package but what her alter ego in the form of Naagin Ki Naani had proved was that if different parts of her body were taken exclusively, then it could drive men crazy. At least she had driven 500K crazy for sure, so far. She could live with that.

The driver pulled the car into a petrol pump. He switched the engine off and stepped out. Falak got down as well. Nityami followed suit. She hated that about herself. She was all about herd mentality. If two or at least one of them were sitting, she wouldn't have stepped out.

Stepping out, the first thing she did was take a deep breath of the chilly air. It freshened her to her core. She saw Falak going inside the washroom. She thought it was a good idea for she didn't know whether they would be stopping in between. Nityami walked towards the washroom, entered and saw Falak standing there.

'Good you came,' said Falak.

'What happened?'

'The door doesn't have a knob. Could you please stand outside? I'll stand for you.'

I'll stand for you . . . the words hit her though Nityami knew they were said casually. Nobody had said that to her before. Not even casually.

'Sure.' Nityami waited till Falak answered nature's call, after which Falak stood on watch outside. As Nityami came out, she thrust her hand forward to Falak.

'Nityami Thakur.'

'Falak Sultana.'

They shook hands. Then both saw the driver waving at them.

As they settled in the car, Nityami took out a bottle of perfume and without warning anyone, sprayed it all over. Falak immediately sneezed.

'Sorry, I have allergies to these,' Falak said, sneezing again.

The driver switched off the engine. Nityami understood he was being superstitious.

'I'm sorry, I should have asked,' Nityami said.

They waited for a few minutes with the windows of the car open so the fragrance would waft outside.

'Did you realize how many times we have said sorry to each other already?' Falak asked with an amused face.

'I know, right? It's as if we are apologizing to each other for all the deeds of our past lives.'

'Yeah, right. Though there's no past or future lives in our belief, but I do get your point.'

'I'm from Bhopal and you are?'

The driver interjected saying, 'Madam, we should leave now. I'm starting the engine. Please don't sneeze in the next few seconds. Then feel free to.'

'Yes, please, let's go,' Nityami said. Because of the stopover, the reach time was back to three hours with some traffic at a few points on the GPS map. The car hit the road while the girls preferred to keep the windows open.

'I'm from Bhopal and you?' Nityami asked again.

'Mumbai,' Falak said. She didn't know if she should talk much after what she had pulled off and was running from.

The mention of Mumbai brought back memories of her friend and her cheating boyfriend. Neither cared to remain in touch after that. Nityami only hoped her friend saw the truth and came out of denial. But then even if she didn't, it wasn't her business.

'I've been to Mumbai once. It's a restless city.'

Falak looked at her, gave a tight smile, then turned her face away—the best way Falak could tell her she wasn't interested in where Nityami had been. Falak had killed two people and was on the run. Nityami's life couldn't have been more interesting than Falak's. Not even in her dreams.

To ensure that Nityami didn't ask her any more questions, Falak pretended to fall asleep, switching her phone off first. Nityami didn't realize it at all. She thought Falak was tired. She too switched her music on and dozed off again. It was early evening when they reached Hotel High Top. The driver brought Nityami to her location first because Falak had not given him any drop location, except that she wanted to be driven to Gangtok. The girls were tired from sitting for so long. Nityami got down and stretched. She bent forward and looking at Falak asked, 'Which hotel are you putting up at?'

Falak glanced at her and said, 'I haven't booked a hotel. I'll figure.'

The last bit told Nityami that Falak was perhaps a reserved person and wasn't interested in keeping in touch. *Who doesn't book and come on a SOLO trip?* Nityami thought and smiled at Falak, 'Take care.'

'You too.'

Falak checked her phone while the driver went to help Nityami with her luggage. He came back to the car in some time.

'Where should I drop you, madam?'

'I'll get down here only,' Falak said, and paying the driver the balance in cash, stepped out. By then she had figured the area had a lot of hotels.

Falak walked towards the nearest hotel following the GPS on her phone. Two hours later, Falak found herself back at the reception of Hotel High Top. For no other hotel in the vicinity had any rooms left. And she prayed at least this one would have one.

*

2

Lying on the bed in her hotel room, Nityami laughed out loud thinking how it wasn't the first time she was in a hotel bed alone. The last time she was like this was in the OYO room booked by the one whom she had already taught a lesson. But this was slightly different. For the first time in life, Nityami had travelled alone. Her parents and Hemant both thought she was in Kolkata but she wasn't. She felt a new sense of excitement within. Multiple times after checking in, Nityami kept moving out of her hotel room. A little sound outside and she would open the door. Then realized what she was doing was stupid. She wanted to share this excitement but it couldn't be with just any stranger. She took her phone out but found nobody with whom she could share this. What a sad life she was living, she thought. It never occurred to her before because she was living within the bubble of a daily routine. This solo trip now gave her the chance of being a third person in her own life. It was such a Catch-22. If you have people in your life, you'll have expectations from them. And if they don't live up to them, you feel disappointed. When you don't have anyone in your life to talk to in moments like these, loneliness seems to be the deadliest situation ever. All she had in the room for company was a TV set which, when she switched it on, only telecast news channels. How wonderful it would be, Nityami thought, to meet new people every day and not have to see them tomorrow. Much like people had a one-night stand but that was for sex. *What about an emotional hook-up?* Was there a way to have a one-night stand emotionally, talk your heart out and then step into tomorrow to meet another person? This way, there would be no expectations nor would there be any loneliness. Nityami burst out laughing a minute later, thinking that so many things would have been sorted—but then, whoever created humans wanted to have fun at their expense. Hence, the complications and humans' innate nature to fall for complications. Nityami decided to rest her thoughts and have her dinner at the in-house restaurant on the terrace.

As Nityami was having the lip-smacking local food, sitting alone by a window, she noticed there weren't many people around. As the waiter came up and placed a glass of lemonade on her table, she asked him, 'Is the hotel not full?'

'It is, madam.'

'Then I think I'm the only one having dinner at this time.'

'No, madam. This is the right time but most of the people have dinner outside.'

Most of the people . . . people with family, friends or a spouse. Obviously, why would they sit here and dine when there were places to visit? Suddenly, the food didn't taste as good as it was up until then. She had a few more spoonfuls and then left it. She picked up the lemonade glass and stepped out of the restaurant after telling the waiter to bill the dinner to her room.

As she stood on the terrace—technically on the third floor—she could see faint outlines of mountains in the distance. The chill in the air was constant while there was silence all around. The only sound that was coming . . . Nityami looked down. There was a car parking within the hotel premises. And beside one of the cars, she noticed the girl with whom she had travelled in the cab. What was her name? Nityami tried recalling it and decided to approach her.

'Sultana!' Nityami said, reaching downstairs. Falak had just ended her call with Razia. She turned to notice Nityami. She remembered her name.

'Nityami. My name is Falak, though.'

'Falak. I'm sorry, I just remembered Sultana.'

'Let's not start competing on the I-am-sorry part again.'

Nityami smiled.

'You putting up in this hotel?'

'Yes. I tried all the other hotels in the vicinity but only this one had one room left. I guess it's on-season time.'

'I guess so, too. But honestly, I didn't even know which season it was. I always prefer to do my tickets beforehand,' Nityami said with confidence.

'You travel alone a lot?' Falak asked, unintentionally puncturing Nityami's confidence.

'Well, yes, I do. This is my tenth solo trip.' Nityami felt a knot in her throat while lying but somehow, being cool in front of the stranger seemed more important.

'Wow. I like that.'

'Don't you travel solo much?' Nityami asked.

'No,' Falak said and looked around.

'We can sit there.' Falak gestured towards a corner where a bonfire was lit for the guests, with chairs around. Nobody was sitting there. Falak and Nityami sat down. The latter was still sipping her lemonade.

'Is it any good?' Falak asked.

'It's okay. I had some local food here so I needed something to get me the necessary burp,' Nityami was being honest here.

'I've something that suits the place, actually.' Falak took out a bottle of Old Monk from her bag.

'I've mixed some water in it already.' She gulped a little down and handed the bottle over to Nityami. She took the bottle, emptied the little lemonade in her glass on the ground below and poured the Old Monk into her glass.

'I can't gulp from bottles.'

'That's all right. My religion doesn't allow this, but I'm having this more as a medicine since I catch cold easily.'

'Alcohol as medicine. Wow, I'm hearing that for the first time. I'm not sure of my religion but my society definitely doesn't like girls drinking. But then, I don't give a damn any more.' Nityami raised her glass while Falak raised her bottle in cheers mode.

'What brings you here? Vacay?' Falak asked. She noticed there was something genuine about Nityami that made her feel comfortable. The genuineness also branched out to give a harmless vibe, which drew Falak.

Nityami had finished the first peg bottoms-up. She took the bottle again and poured herself another peg. Falak was right, she thought, what lemonade-shit was I drinking being in Gangtok? This is the real deal!

'Total vacation. Wanted to take a break from work. What about you?'

'Wanted to take a break from life,' Falak said. Nityami gave her a sharp glance. As if sensing where she was coming from.

A guy approached them.

'Hello ladies, I am Jack.' The guy was from the north-eastern part of India, looked insanely cute and had a guitar with him.

'Are you looking for Daniels, Jack?' Falak asked. Jack got her joke and laughed while Nityami laughed only because she didn't want to be left behind. She didn't know Jack Daniels was a whisky brand.

'I'm from the hotel, ladies. Here to entertain the guests. May I play something for you?' Jack asked.

Those words brought a memory to Falak. She smiled, thinking about the time when, on stage in college, Vedant was playing the guitar. And one of the songs he played was her request. Falak told Jack to play the same Hindi song. As Jack started playing, Nityami quipped, 'That's one of my personal faves!'

As the song played on, Nityami poured herself more Old Monk and started daydreaming about the moment she would meet Vedant, perhaps in twenty-four hours. Jack kept playing one song after the other, as requested by the girls, and before Nityami knew it, she finished the Old Monk. And then, while clapping as Jack ended his seventh song, she fell from the chair.

All the hotel staff were male so it was Falak who took Nityami inside. Her room number was 9 while Falak's was 13. As the two stepped on to the floor where their rooms were, Nityami, trying hard to keep her eyes open, said, 'I can go from here.'

'You sure?'

'Absolutely. I'm used to it,' Nityami said.

'Okay.' Falak left her outside room number 9 and entered her own room. Nityami thought Falak was still there. She said, 'Thanks, Sultana.' And turned, in the process, facing the other way, towards the room opposite. She tried unlocking the door with her key. This wasn't a hotel that had card keys. The door was suddenly opened from the inside. Nityami looked up and thought it was the day she had reached the OYO room and Raghav had opened the door. There was an instant rush of anger which made Nityami slap the guy hard.

'What the hell!' said the man who opened the door. His girlfriend came out, pushing him aside, sensing something was wrong. Nityami ignored the man and looked at the girl.

'You're with an asshole. I hope you know that. And he may fuck you but he will never stand up for you when his parents accuse you of being a slut.'

The girlfriend frowned and looked at the guy, 'How does she know about your parents?'

'I don't know. I'm seeing this girl for the first time. I swear.'

By then, Falak came out of her room out of curiosity hearing the verbal chaos. She was in two minds whether she should step in or not. She was about to close her door but she heard the girl charge Nityami with abuses since she had slapped her guy. Realizing this would go on and she would get no sleep, which she desperately wanted, Falak simply walked up to Nityami.

'Please excuse her. She is my friend. She is a man-hater for some personal reasons. And she is drunk. Please excuse her.' Saying so, Falak pulled Nityami away, took the key from her hand, unlocked the door of room no. 9 and, placing her on the bed, left the room.

When she retired to her own room, Falak understood that Nityami had lied to her about her solo travels. Someone who can't handle Old Monk can't be solo travelling like this, she concluded and lay on her bed wondering what Razia must be up to in Delhi before exhaustion lulled her to sleep.

*

3

Falak woke up to knocking at her door. *Are the police here?* She sat up on the bed with a start. The same thing had happened in the nightmare she had, which had woken her up around 3 a.m. that very night. She dreamt that the Delhi police had figured Zamaan and Wasim were actually murdered by Falak in cold blood and she was going to be arrested for it. The police had come down right to her hotel room, pulled her out, handcuffed her and taken her straight to jail. The images she saw in the dream—of the police—their brutality, the jail—were all an amalgamation of film images she had seen, with her face instead of the actors'. Not that she had not herself gone to a police station in real life, thanks to Wasim. But it was never for her or even because of her. When she woke up, all startled, realizing it was all a dream, Falak immediately called Razia up.

'All good?' Falak, since the time she ran away from Delhi, asked the same thing every time she called Razia. That night, knowing Zamaan was dead while she hoped Wasim must have eaten the parathas that she prepared, she exactly didn't know where she was heading from Nizamuddin railway station. The only good thing she did was, apart from the note she had kept on Zamaan addressed to Razia, she had also kept a separate note for Wasim, pressed in his palm, which was a suicide note where she had mentioned the following:

I'm killing myself. Falak, my girlfriend, has left me. I don't even know if she is dead or alive. All this because her father beat her up after discovering our clandestine affair. He was opposed to it. I say opposed because I've killed him as well. I mixed rat poison in the parathas which I gave him and then I ate the same. I don't want anyone to think anything otherwise. And if possible please tell my girlfriend I loved her. – Wasim.

Hoping she'd pulled off a perfect murder, Falak took the first train that was waiting to leave from the Nizamuddin Railway Station. It was after an hour later, sitting on the only empty seat she had found on the train, she learnt from a co-passenger that the destination of the train was Kolkata. She went to the bathroom only to throw her SIM card down the toilet. At that point in time, all she had in mind was to go far away from Delhi. The guilt was not about poisoning her father or boyfriend, the guilt was that she had to leave Razia behind. There was no way both could have run away, otherwise, more than the police, everyone else in the family would have had their doubts.

After reaching Kolkata, the first thing Falak did was buy a new SIM. She put it in her old phone and immediately called up Razia. The latter was relieved hearing Falak's voice. For the first minute, both simply heard each other's silent tears. Then Razia told her that the funeral preparations of her Abbu had already begun.

'Did the police come?' Falak asked.

'Yes, they did. Good you didn't tell me about Wasim's suicide letter.'

'Why?'

'My shock when the police told me about it was damn genuine. They understood I wasn't involved and probably what was written in the suicide letter was true.'

'Not that I thought about it but it's good to know something went our way. All I was confident of was they wouldn't have any written material to match Wasim's handwriting.'

'Now I'm sure they didn't because they were asking me about Wasim's parents for last rites.'

'Great.'

'I'll call you soon. Don't give my number to anybody.'

'Of course, I won't. But where are you? Do you have money?' asked a concerned Razia.

'I'm in Kolkata. I took out most of my savings from an ATM in Nizamuddin.'

'Kolkata? Do you know anyone there?' Razia asked.

Falak didn't think twice before replying, 'No.'

It was the truth that Falak knew nobody in Kolkata. It was the first time she had actually been there. Moving out of the busy Howrah Station, she bought herself a plate of puri-sabzi and hogged it up in no time. After she drank some water and felt her soul come alive again, she thought about what her next step should be.

Falak called her brother, Imtiaz, and cried on the phone, sharing their father's death. She didn't mention Wasim to him.

'I'm going to Delhi soon. I'll see you there,' Imtiaz said.

'I'll try to be here, bhai, but it looks difficult,' Falak said.

'Where are you going?'

'I'm looking for a job in Bengaluru. I'll stay there only.'

'That's good. Earn and live your own life.'

For the first time, Falak felt her brother talked some sense. Maybe the world was making him wiser.

'But I'm thinking,' Imtiaz continued, 'it's better Razia stays in Delhi itself. I can't live with her here in Mumbai.'

'I understand. Let her remain in Delhi only. Anyway, I don't like her,' Falak lied. She knew it was better for Razia to stay in Delhi.

'I don't even know her. Nor am I interested.'

'Let everyone go to hell. You take care, bhai, I'll come to Mumbai soon and meet you.'

'You too take care.'

Falak spent a day in Kolkata and realized that living in a big city would make her lose all her savings very soon, considering her per-day expenses. All she had to do was stay away for a week. And then go back to Delhi, complete her MBA, secure a job and carry on with life, finally. Falak googled cheap places to visit from Kolkata and figured Sikkim was not only a place that fit into her budget but also the kind of soulful place where she could reflect on her life a little.

As the knocking on the door began again, Falak got down from her bed and, on high alert, went near the door and asked in a suspicious tone, 'Who is it?'

'Nityami,' a voice answered. Falak relaxed, rolling her eyes, and opened the door.

'I know I shouldn't say it but I'm sorry.' Nityami had a guilty look on her face. Falak could see she must have rehearsed the line multiple times before because of the self-conscious look on her face.

'I'm surprised you remember,' Falak said.

'I do,' Nityami said. Then looking straight at Falak, she added, 'Well, I didn't. All I remembered was I slapped someone. Then I vaguely recall I was with you so I thought I had slapped you. I had to apologize.'

Falak was amused.

'Did I really slap you?'

'No. But come in first,' Falak said. As Nityami stepped inside the room, Falak looked out. Everything seemed normal. She let out a sigh of relief and closed the door.

'Coffee?' Falak asked, going towards the electric kettle in the room.

'Sure,' Nityami said eagerly. Nobody had asked her for coffee, or for that matter anything, in that deeply friendly tone in a long time.

In no time, Falak made two mugs of coffee. She sat on the bed while Nityami had taken the bamboo chair in the room. In the next two minutes, Falak narrated to her what had actually transpired last night in the floor lobby.

'Oh god!' Nityami was visibly embarrassed as she face-palmed herself.

'You can't handle alcohol, so why did you drink so much?'

'I can't handle a lot of things, actually,' Nityami muttered to herself, then removed her hand from her face and took a gulp of the hot coffee. As the coffee warmed her within, she looked up at Falak. 'I lied to you. I don't travel solo. In fact, this is my first time.'

'I guessed that.'

Nityami's face fell.

'What happened?'

'That's my eternal problem. I'm bloody obvious. There's nothing unpredictable about me.'

'That slap was unpredictable,' Falak said matter-of-factly. It made Nityami shift on her seat; her curiosity aroused.

'Really? Did I hit the guy hard?'

'Hard enough for his girlfriend to come out and confront you.'

'Damn. This embarrassment isn't ending. How did you pacify them?'

'I told them you're a man-hater.'

Nityami's jaw dropped.

'I've been abused with a lot of things but not that.'

'That's not an abuse, really. It's just being practical. I don't think there are enough men left who deserve full-blown romantic surrender from us.'

Nityami let out a deep sigh.

'How true. And the ones who get dedicated men are the ones who turn out to be bitches . . .'

'Irony of life,' Falak lamented.

The irony is, Nityami pondered, *I lied to my parents and to the guy who could well be a good prospect as my life partner and came here to clear my confusion. Why would my batchmate think Vedant was dating me? Did he really mention my name? And also, to check if there indeed was any chance. Chance! The soul of any love story.*

The silence that followed told Falak that she should change the topic.

'So, did you come here with a plan?' After hearing Nityami's plans, Falak thought she could also decide whether to stay in Gangtok or go further into the interiors.

'I'm going to Gurudongmar Lake,' Nityami said. 'I'll take a cab today after checking out from here. But I guess I need to wait until the night for him.'

'For him?'

'Oops, to reach the lake,' Nityami said. They still hadn't reached that stage where Nityami thought of sharing her actual motive to reach Gurudongmar.

'Why a night move?'

'I need to stay overnight in Lachen and then go there. What's your plan?'

'One second.' Falak excused herself and went to the washroom. She sat on the toilet seat and googled Lachen. A quick look told her it was just the kind of town she should be in. Falak came out of the washroom and said, 'Guess what? Even I'm going to Lachen.'

'Oh, wonderful. We can share the cab.'

'Absolutely.'

The girls decided to freshen up and meet at the terrace restaurant for breakfast. Nityami reached the restaurant first. From there, she called her parents and then Hemant. She filled them in on all her imaginary goings-on. The moment her parents asked her to WhatsApp some pictures so her mother could forward them to her ladies' WhatsApp groups, for some ego-bloating showing off to others that her daughter was also going places, Nityami quickly ended the call.

Falak came up with her small backpack. Nityami glanced at it, then looked at all the luggage she had brought up.

'You have to teach me how you manage to travel so light,' Nityami said.

'Sure.' *Kill people and run. You'll automatically know how to travel light*, Falak thought. 'I learnt it from my mother,' Falak lied.

The two girls sat down for breakfast. While Nityami's breakfast was included in the room booking price, Falak had to pay for hers. In between their breakfast, Falak's phone rang; it was Razia. She picked up the phone immediately and said, 'I'll call you later.' And ended the call. Nityami hadn't seen whose call it was, but she assumed it must have been Falak's boyfriend. And she didn't want to talk to him in her presence. But she also remembered her boyfriend was also a fan of Naagin Ki Naani. Before coming to the terrace for breakfast, Nityami had uploaded a fresh reel where she had exposed her thighs against the windows and captured the gooseflesh triggered by the cold outside. Now she wondered that, of all the men who must have liked the reel, was one Falak's boyfriend too?

Nityami booked the cab for both of them. Once they were done with breakfast, the girls were told by the hotel staff that their cab was waiting outside the hotel. They were ready to go to Lachen.

*

4

Nityami was having some breathing problems as their car started the ascent. Lachen was 10,000 feet above sea level. Falak, however, sat with great enthusiasm. The breathtaking view of the snow-capped mountains in the distance, as their car manoeuvred within the lap of the valley, was something she was seeing for the first time in her life. What was she doing till now? Just fighting her everyday battles to exist? Looking at the beatific nature all around, Falak realized it was so important to travel. To venture out. To *leave*. If you don't leave, you won't learn about the universe through your own journey. It's like, to understand the ocean, you have to dive deep inside one single drop. And perhaps only after you leave, are you able to collect enough soul-dust to understand the value of settling down.

The rebellious nature that Falak already possessed got new wings, it seemed to her. Without caring much about whether the cold weather would affect her, Falak opened the car's window and popped her head out. She felt like crying. It had taken killing her father and boyfriend for her to reach here. Had she not done what she had, what would her life have been like? Her father would, in all probability, have busted her lies. Forced her to stop going to her MBA college, stopped her tiffin service thus terminating her independent life and would have compelled her to marry someone whom she either didn't know at all or knew enough to have hated the person. Just like what happened to Razia. The very fact that she always supported her was because Falak was just one step ahead of her. Had she been on the same point, her dreams too would have been squashed like mosquitoes. That's how men, she knew, saw a female's dreams. Like an irksome mosquito that had to be killed before it sucked the blood out of patriarchy. She felt sorry for herself for sustaining Wasim's gender-conditioned wrath. She should have shown zero tolerance and moved out when he forced her sexually for the first time. She should have stood against her father the day he said he wouldn't spend a single buck for her education. There were so many other instances and all of them were coming back to her one by one as the icy-cold wind hit her face. And funnily enough, in hindsight, she realized she had so many options to handle them but when they were happening, she was convinced there was only one way to react: to suffer them.

Sitting on the other side, Nityami was feeling butterflies in her stomach. There was literally one day between Vedant and her. And the mystery of why he had been speaking her name. But the closer she got, the more a fear gripped her as well. If she was honest with herself, she wasn't going to Gurudongmar to only meet Vedant after years. She was seeking him out for herself. She didn't know him much as an adult because her interactions with Vedant had happened only at school, from where on she only had an impression of him in her mind and heart. And something visceral told her he wasn't any different from that. The seeking was also to check whether she felt the same about him. Whether the fact that she fell in love with him in school was just one of those teenage things that happened to almost everyone in varying degrees at that age or if coming across each other, then and now, would have a deeper and more lasting role.

The car had to be stopped a good seven times in between because Nityami had serious motion sickness.

'Don't want to use that expression but I'm really very sorry,' she told Falak. 'I never knew I had such bad motion sickness.'

'It's okay. We all don't know a lot of things about ourselves until we move out of our comfort zone.'

'How true!' With the passing of time, Nityami had started to like Falak.

After Nityami threw up for the seventh time, she felt her intestines would come out if she did it once more. All her breakfast was out. Her head was reeling.

'I think my BP is low,' Nityami blurted out, gasping for air a little.

'Are you a BP patient?'

'No, but right now, I can feel my head reeling like anything. Maybe I vomited out a lot of salt, that's why this is happening.'

'Could be. But I don't think there's any doctor nearby till we reach Lachen.'

'I can wait. I just don't want to die,' Nityami said, feeling scared.

'Shut up. You'll be all right,' Falak assured her and kept clasping her hand for warmth. It provided the much-needed assurance for Nityami.

Some 17 km from Lachen, their car came to an abrupt halt. Nityami was asleep. Falak was too, but she woke up with the jolt she felt. She noticed the driver had moved out of the car already. A glance at Nityami told her she was sound asleep. When the driver didn't come back in, Falak decided to step out.

She went in front where the driver was standing with the bonnet open.

'What happened?'

'Not sure, madam.'

Falak realized it would take time to fix the problem. She heard the car's door open and then shut. The next second Nityami was there by her side, blocking a yawn.

'How did you know I wanted to pee?' she asked.

Falak frowned, 'We stopped because there's something wrong with the car.'

'Oh!' The residual sleep flew off Nityami's face. 'But I want to pee anyway.'

She looked around.

'There, behind that boulder,' Falak said. She watched Nityami go a little towards the boulder's direction, then stop and turn to look at Falak.

'Do you mind if you could stand for me?'

'Sure,' Falak said and joined her.

The boulder was around 600 metres from the road. Once Nityami was done, she noticed there was no Falak.

'Falak!' she screamed out. Only to hear a whistle. She noticed, to her relief, that Falak was sitting on the boulder above.

'I also want to come up there.'

'Then come up.'

'How?'

'Figure out.'

Two minutes later, Nityami managed to climb the boulder and sit beside Falak. She was huffing and puffing for air.

'I've become so soft. I have to go to the gym once I'm back home.'

Falak didn't respond. Nityami observed she was in some kind of trance.

'That mountain in the distance, this vastness around . . . it makes you and your problems so small, so insignificant isn't it?'

Nityami looked ahead and for a few seconds soaked in the view as she thought over what Falak had said.

Falak is right, Nityami thought, the view was making her relook at her own existence. Nature is the supreme boss. And everything else is a subset of it going around, performing roles as nature has given them. There was both a magic and a mystery in it. A magic whose trick can't be learnt, no matter how high one's spiritual quotient is. A mystery which can't be deciphered no matter the progress of science.

'And yet we, in our head, have a magnified view of our problems. It's we who convince ourselves how big our problems are.'

Falak glanced at Nityami and asked, 'What's that one thing you would have corrected about your life, if given the power?'

Nityami thought for quite some time without speaking. Falak was in no hurry either.

Maybe the Raghav incident, maybe my encounter with Aashiq, maybe proposing to Vedant, maybe moving out of Bhopal or even India for job opportunities, maybe . . . and suddenly Nityami realized how shallow she was being. All those 'maybes' were about others. Perhaps what Falak asked wasn't about adding or deleting people from one's life, but about some inward correction. Thinking hard on this line, Nityami finally came up with an answer.

'I would have corrected myself. I don't call a spade a spade at times. Sometimes it's emotional pressure, sometimes it's fear of the future and at times, it's just conditioning. I shouldn't have succumbed to it.' A pause later she asked, 'What about you?'

Falak's reply came instantly.

'This nature of mine which remains in-between. I always knew what I should do and yet I chose to remain chained. And now it's too late.'

'Too late? Why? I guess you are younger than me,' Nityami said.

Falak glanced at her once, quickly calculating if she should tell her everything but in a split second decided otherwise.

'That should tell you all that I may have gone through till now.'

Nityami considered what Falak said and then smirked saying, 'I'm so happy I made this trip. I've already realized when you move out of your comfort zone, you understand what people are going through. And probably what you are going through is nothing compared to that.'

There was prolonged silence. Then Nityami asked Falak, 'Has anyone broken your heart, ever?'

Falak shook her head and said, 'No.'

The innocence in Nityami made her take pride in the fact that she had felt heartbreak more than Falak. Though she wasn't asked, Nityami herself said, 'I have had numerous heartbreaks. And it's not the heartbreak which is a problem. It is the version of the person within you which is left behind after the heartbreak, which is. You just don't know what to do. It punctures your confidence, belittles your conviction, tells you that you can't make good choices. Basically, a heartbreak is an exercise in regressing your personality. It just fuses the light in you, one day at a time. So, you are lucky nobody broke your heart, Falak.'

'I meant no person broke my heart, ever.'

Falak glanced at Nityami. The latter could notice her eyes going faintly moist. That's a good thing, Nityami thought.

'You want someone to? As I said, it's not a . . .' she couldn't finish.

'Life broke my heart from the time I gained my senses,' Falak said aloud, trying hard but not being able to stop the choking in her voice.

'It's not me, but you who are lucky. A heart broken by a person can still be mended. But a heart broken by life . . . it's a long, long wait. Most of it a hopeless one.'

Nityami wanted to probe her more about it but a different voice stopped her.

'Madam! The car is ready to go.'

The girls heard the driver shout out to them. Followed by the car's horn.

5

They finally reached Lachen. Nityami had booked a homestay. The driver helped them figure out where exactly it was. They met the landlord who welcomed them wholeheartedly.

'Myself Tshering. I have been waiting for you since morning,' Tshering said, looking at Nityami.

'Thanks,' a weak Nityami said. Falak was still holding her hand. Tshering noticed it and said, 'I thought you would be staying alone. Are you two a couple?'

The moment the girls realized what Tshering was hinting at, they jerked away each other's hands.

'No. We are . . .' Nityami started.

'Travel mates,' Falak completed.

'Right,' Nityami added.

'I was asking because if you were a couple, I would have given you a bigger room. I have two rooms. The bigger one is occupied.'

'No worries. We will only need the room for the night. Tomorrow I'm going to Gurudongmar Lake; she may stay on,' Nityami said.

'That's wonderful. My boy will take your luggage. I just need one ID each.'

'Sure.'

The girls gave their IDs to Tshering, who whistled once. Before the girls could realize why he did so, they both noticed a snow dog running up to them from some distance away.

'Romeo will take you to your room,' Tshering said and took out a set of keys. The dog—Romeo—grabbed the keys between his teeth and ran ahead while the girls followed.

Romeo stood in front of a room. It was opposite to another one, which was the bigger room. Falak took the keys from Romeo, caressed his forehead and unlocked the door. As the girls entered, they noticed that the room was just big enough for two people. But then, it was a matter of one night, the girls thought, and neither complained. Romeo went to a heater, then inside the washroom to show the immersion rod and finally drew the curtain with his teeth. The view was breathtaking. Since it was dusk, the distant mountains were a little hazy. The girls couldn't wait for morning to arrive.

As the luggage came in and the girls had just locked themselves in the room, there was a knock on the door. It was Tshering. He gave Falak, who had opened the door, a menu.

'What will you have for dinner?'

Falak checked the menu given to her. There were three items in all on it:

Classic Maggi Noodles.

Cheese Maggi Noodles.

Egg Maggi Noodles.

'You have such a long list of options,' Falak said sarcastically. Tshering took it in his stride.

'Show me,' Nityami said. Falak tossed the menu to her. She saw the list and understood why Falak had said what she did.

'I'll take the classic Maggi Noodles,' Nityami said.

'Please make that two,' Falak told Tshering. He went away, taking the menu with him. Falak hadn't returned Razia's call since the morning. She excused herself, saying there was no network on her phone and she needed to go outside to talk.

'You can use mine. I have full network,' Nityami said. She didn't want Falak to leave her alone in the room. It was a far-from-neatly-done hotel room and she was scared.

'I'm here only. A shout away.'

Falak went out and closed the door behind her. She called Razia.

'How's it going?'

'All good, by Allah's wish. You tell me, where are you?'

'In a small town in Sikkim.'

'Sikkim? How did you reach there?'

'Forget it. When is Abbu's funeral?'

'Tomorrow. All the preparations are done.'

'What about Wasim?'

'His is the day after since the police had taken his body to the morgue where his parents identified him.'

'Hmm.'

'I miss you, Falak. When will we meet?'

'I miss you too. This place is so amazing. Just the type where people like us should come and stay for some time. We will surely come here together.'

'Can hardly wait for it.'

'You know, while being driven here, I felt how small our battles are in front of nature and yet we keep whining, complaining and cribbing. We never relax and just be. It's just one life. There's so much to do apart from just bother ourselves with minuscule and unimportant things.'

'Sounds like someone has suddenly grown up.'

'I told you I met this girl on the trip, Nityami. She is so innocent and funny at times. Thank God I got her, else this would have been a really lonely trip.'

'This isn't a trip, Falak. You shouldn't have done what you did in the first place. Though I know why you did it, but . . .'

'It's done now, Razia sweety. There's no point talking about it. And don't worry, I'm not a psycho serial killer who will go on adding rat poison in parathas. By the way, parathas remind me—if it's possible, please handle the tiffin service for my clients. I'll WhatsApp you their phone numbers.'

'Yes, I was going to remind you of that. Message me the numbers. I'll try my best so that by the time you return, you still have your clients.'

'I never told you how much I love you, Razia sweety.'

'Let's say that to each other once you are back. So badly waiting to see you.'

'So am I.' After a pause, Falak said in a serious tone, 'A burden is off my chest.'

'Which burden?'

'With Abbu no more, I don't have to call you Ammi,' Falak laughed out loud. So did Razia.

'And with your Abbu gone, I can message Furkan without feeling guilty.'

'Oh yes!' Falak sounded surprised in a pleasant way. 'See, one action of mine and so many good things happening. How can it be a bad act?'

It was then that Falak saw him. It was slightly dark so she wasn't sure. But the man looked like him. Falak didn't move. He was at some distance inside an SUV. He stepped out after parking it and then came up. As he moved past her, Falak was sure it was him. For a moment, things seemed to move in slow motion. Then she got her voice back, hearing Razia on the other end.

'Raziaaa!'

'What happened?'

'I'll call you soon.' Falak ended the call and followed the man. She saw him unlock the room opposite theirs and enter it.

Falak came rushing inside her room. She checked herself in the mirror on the wall. It was only a bust-length mirror. This was the first time since she left Delhi that she looked at her reflection with interest. If it was really him, she wasn't going to check on him looking absolutely ordinary. She quickly washed her face, applied a little bit of lipstick, rubbed her lips together; then combed her hair and redid the kohl in her eyes. She even took out a pair of earrings from her bag and put them on. They were Razia's. Falak used to wear them often but she had removed them while boarding the train from Nizamuddin to avoid unnecessary attention since they were of pure gold. Nityami was lying under the blanket watching her. She didn't have the energy to get up. All this time lying alone in the room, she was cursing her luck that she would in all probability meet Vedant the next day looking weak and drained. She was looking forward to a good night's sleep after dinner so at least she could wake up fresh. The dinner was yet to come, though.

'Does Bumble work here? Did you match with someone? Or is there a hot guy around?' Nityami asked, seeing an unprecedented urgency in Falak to look good. Falak turned back and gave her a warm smile. The kind she hadn't yet seen on Falak's face.

'I just saw the love of my life, Vedant Kaushal.'

'That's wonderful,' Nityami said with a smile. Then the smile disappeared abruptly.

'Wait, what? Who? Where? How?' Nityami had never asked so many questions in one go.

*

6

'I'll be back. Then I'll tell you everything,' Falak said and before Nityami could react, went out of the room.

What just happened? Nityami, lying flat on the bed, didn't know how to react. *Was it a coincidence? Vedant Kaushal? Seriously? Did she say that name? How would she know Vedant? Was she here secretly seeking Vedant just like her? The one girl she thought was a great travel partner was actually her competition?* Nityami couldn't take the storm of questions hovering in her mind. She sat up, though feeling weaker.

Nityami had no option but to wait for Falak to return. Then something struck her. *What if it was indeed her Vedant Kaushal?* Nityami pulled herself out of the bed and went to the bust-length mirror in the room to put on some make-up. If this was a war over Vedant Kaushal, Nityami thought, looking at her reflection in the mirror, then looking better than Falak was her best weapon going forward. She, after, was Naagin Ki Naani as well. And it was high time the vengeful Naagin came out from the reel world to the real one.

Falak stood in front of the room in which she saw Vedant stepping in. She didn't know if he was staying there all alone.

Or with family . . . or spouse. It would be serious to barge in and disturb their privacy if he was there with his wife or girlfriend or family. Falak was in two minds. Suddenly, Romeo appeared, wagging his tail. He was a friendly Husky. Falak had an idea. Instead of knocking on the door, she went to Tshering. He had built this house as a homestay while he stayed with his family in the adjacent one.

'Sorry to disturb you, Tshering,' Falak said.

'The noodles are almost ready,' Tshering said, seeing Falak. His last guest had left angry because he had taken time to serve him the food. Tshering didn't want a repeat of this, for these days people had the power of the Internet where the reviews were taken seriously.

'That's great. Also, I just wanted to know, who is staying in the bigger room?'

'Why, what happened?' Tshering sensed some problem.

'Nothing. I think the person is an old friend but I'm not sure, so I was asking.'

'His name is Vedant Kaushal.'

A smile appeared on Falak's face. A knot in her stomach. A weakness in her knees. And her heart missed a beat. Tshering figured she knew him.

'Is he here alone or with . . .'

'Alone.'

The smile stretched into a beamer for Falak.

'Thanks, Tshering.'

Falak went back with a spring in her step, and standing in front of the bigger room, took a deep breath. She was about to knock when she heard Nityami call out from right behind her.

'Falak, you've been standing here since you came out of our room?'

'No. Why?' Falak found Nityami's patronizing tone a little off.

'I'm hungry,' Nityami didn't know how to ask her straight whether she meant the same Vedant Kaushal that she knew.

'I checked with Tshering. He will be here with the noodles any time now.'

'Great. Come, let's wait together then,' Nityami said, turned and realized she was the only one who wanted to be in the room.

'You wait inside, I'll be there soon.' As Falak said so, Nityami realized she was up to something that she wanted to hide from her. Something related to Vedant Kaushal. Not finding any other excuse to delay Falak from doing whatever she wanted to do, Nityami went inside the room, closed the door but put her ear to it to catch what was actually up.

Convinced Nityami wouldn't be back, Falak took another deep breath and was about to knock on the bigger room's door, when Tshering called out this time.

'Hot steaming noodles are ready, madam.' Tshering came up to Falak. Their room door opened and Nityami came out with a smile.

'Wow, I can't wait to have it. Let's eat, come.' Nityami took the two bowls from Tshering.

'Thanks, Tshering,' Falak said and realized it was impossible to check on Vedant at that moment. She went inside their room, following Nityami. As she closed the door, she noticed Nityami's make-up.

'You were going out somewhere?' Falak asked, taking a bowl of noodles from her.

'I thought you were. So, I also got ready. Can't live in this room alone. Gives me some scary vibes,' Nityami said.

Falak couldn't stop laughing.

'I wasn't going out. I saw someone whom I knew before. In fact, not just know, I was in love with him.'

Nityami was already feeling a fear growing inside her.

'Oh! That's some coincidence,' Nityami said. She was sifting her wooden fork through the noodles to steam it out. And through the steam going up, she was keeping an eye on Falak.

'I know. So was his coming into my life in the first place. It's funny, but when it happened for the first time, I thought it was all planned . . . but now I agree this is some coincidence.'

'What's his name?' Nityami knew she shouldn't have asked. Not because there was a problem in asking but the answer, she knew, would stop her heart.

'Vedant Kaushal,' came the instant response. The answer made it difficult for Nityami to breathe. *How do I confirm if it's only a name overlap or . . .* Nityami wondered.

'What a coincidence!' Nityami's voice almost jumped out of her.

'What? We talked about coincidences already.' Falak stopped eating her noodles midway. She sensed Nityami had been acting funny since she had gone out to meet Vedant.

'Actually, I didn't tell you before. I'm on a solo trip but I didn't come here with a vacation in mind.'

'Then?' Falak said and thought: *Did she too kill someone?*

'I came here looking for my first love; Vedant Kaushal.'

What? Is she making up this story? was Falak's first reaction.

'When did you meet Vedant?' Falak asked.

Nityami told her side of the story with utmost sincerity and truth. She didn't hide anything. It didn't come naturally to her either. Falak, however, didn't believe any of it. She couldn't. Though the genuineness with which Nityami narrated her story with Vedant hit her hard.

'What if this Vedant is the Vedant you came here looking for?' Falak seemed to be carefully crafting her questions.

'I want to ask him why he had mentioned my name. Does he miss me? Is he single? Can we . . .' Nityami stopped, realizing she was sounding like a sixteen-year-old.

'There's only one way to check. We have to knock on his door.' Falak finished her noodles. A tad too fast.

'But what's your story with him?'

'Well . . .' Falak told her the past in a superficial manner. Nityami was jealous that Falak was ahead of her on the wooing Vedant curve. She had not only proposed to him but he also knew her feelings. That way, he would be happier to see her than Nityami. She felt sad. And defeated.

'You said he had just come in from somewhere. Let's give him time to rest and then let's knock on his door.' Nityami wanted the time for herself. What if he recognized Falak and not her? She would jump into Gurudongmar Lake and kill herself then. Fair plan, Nityami told herself.

'Umm, yeah, fair enough. But it also means you don't have to go to Gurudongmar.'

'Depends,' Nityami said and thought, *It depends on whether he recognizes me*. But then, if his saying-my-name part is true, he would recognize her immediately. And right then, Nityami understood it wasn't about recognizing her any more. The point was, whom would he vibe more with? Both the girls were a blast from Vedant's past. Suddenly, Nityami felt her whole trip, her entire attempt of lying to her parents and Hemant, and coming over here was a big zero.

They heard Tshering talking to someone outside. The girls looked at each other and then, at the same time, scampered to the window. Standing there, they both saw Vedant. Nityami had tears in her eyes on seeing him. He seemed like a vague dream in the distance. Falak had an old smile on her face. The kind which she used to have when looking at Vedant in college. Life had dampened this smile of hers. He felt like a fresh breeze of air in their humid life.

Before the girls could zip the stupid smile on their respective faces and call out or run to him, Vedant Kaushal got into the parked SUV and drove off.

*

7

Both the girls came down running. They caught hold of Tshering, who was downstairs.

'Where did he go?' Falak asked.

'What happened, madam? Did he do anything?'

Yes, he has both our hearts, Nityami thought in a filmi way but was scared of being judged, so she didn't say it aloud.

'We know him from before. Just wanted to meet,' she said instead.

'Are you sure?' Tshering asked.

'Yeah, why?' Falak said, and both the girls exchanged an is-all-well glance.

'He isn't just a guest.'

'Then? The owner?'

Tshering looked at the girls alternately, as if he wasn't sure if he should share something important, and said, 'Meet him first.'

'But where did he go? Don't tell me Gangtok,' Nityami said.

'Gurudongmar Lake.'

'At this hour? Isn't it late?' Nityami was tired and thought it would be better if she met Vedant with a fresh face instead of her exhausted one.

'Where do we get a cab from here?' Falak blurted out.

'Wait, I'll arrange one for both of you. The charges would be . . .'

'I'll handle that,' Nityami said. *If Falak can meet him now, so can I*. It was a 'note-to-self'.

Falak and Nityami didn't wait. The moment the cab arrived half an hour later, they both hopped into it with eagerness and excitement.

'Don't you think Tshering was a little weird concerning Vedant?' Nityami asked.

'For sure he was. Let's meet Vedant and figure out what's happening.'

'Yes.'

The drive from Lachen to Gurudongmar was about two and a half hours long. The road was typical of the mountains but Nityami was more prepared this time; Tshering had got her some medicines from a local doctor so she wouldn't throw up.

After the cab dropped them off, they had to walk for some time before they noticed the SUV in which Vedant had driven off. As the girls walked further, the majestic, almost mythical and breathtakingly beautiful Gurudongmar Lake came into view. The girls glanced at each other to share that they both were mesmerized by its magnificence. And if that wasn't enough, they saw their man sitting with his back to them at the side of the lake.

When they noticed him, they didn't realize the walk to him would be almost a kilometre. By the time they reached him, they were gasping for air.

Some way behind Vedant, the girls stood deciding who should approach him first.

'I'm just wondering if there's a way we could pretend all of this is a coincidence. That I didn't come here knowing that he was here too. It might freak him out,' Nityami said.

'Don't you think you are a little late in thinking about it? He is right there.'

'But he hasn't seen us yet. You have anything in mind?'

'I didn't even know he was here. In fact, the coincidence is the truth in my case.'

She has a point, Nityami thought.

'Then what should we do?' This reached Vedant's ears. He turned to look at the girls. They didn't know whether to smile or wave their hands or act surprised. They both stood like statues. Vedant stood up and came to them. He first looked at Falak. Then at Nityami. His eyes stayed on Nityami longer, as if her face was slowly taking him back in time.

'Falak Sultana, Nityami Thakur,' Vedant said. According to the girls, Vedant was looking like the best-upgraded version of himself. Like how he had been in his early and late teens, but now he had shaped up to his potential. Except, both noticed, his eyes were looking tired. Evidently from sleeplessness.

'How are you, Vedant?' Falak asked. Nityami wanted to ask first but she preferred to revel in his presence. The wallflower in her was taking charge once again like it used to in school. She suddenly turned into this teen girl whose first crush and love was standing in front of her and, instead of talking to him, she was only listening.

'How are you both doing? I never knew you knew each other.'

'I'm good,' Nityami managed to say.

'So am I,' Falak added.

There was an awkward hiatus of a few seconds. Nityami shut the wallflower in her and spoke up.

'I heard from a common friend that you were camping here.'

'Not camping really, but yeah, I come down here because this is Nitya's favourite place.'

Falak could see from the corner of her eye that Nityami was glancing at her.

'Nitya?' Falak asked.

'My girlfriend,' Vedant said with a smile that had long ago injured the girls standing right in front of him. Now the injury opened up for an entirely different reason.

Vedant looked at his watch, which was sounding an alarm. He stopped it and looking at the girls, said, 'Lovely to meet again. See you around, girls.'

They watched Vedant walk away and then disappear into his SUV. The SUV drove off.

'This means Nitya is there with him in the bigger room,' Falak said. Nityami didn't like the fact that she had to repeat things that were unpleasant to her ears. She preferred sitting at the same spot Vedant had been sitting, overlooking the Gurudongmar Lake. There was literally nobody around. She had never been to a place where she couldn't see one single human being anywhere. Feeling the emptiness in the air, she went ahead and sat down on the spot where Vedant had been sitting. Seconds later, she sensed Falak too sitting beside her.

'I know you're more heartbroken than me,' Falak said.

Nityami didn't reply.

'You thought or whoever told you about it also thought that he was saying your name, right?'

Nityami continued to be quiet.

'I'd accepted long ago that I had lost Vedant. This was just a glimmer of hope.' Saying so, Falak too went into silent mode. The chilly wind kept hitting them. After some time, Nityami spoke.

'Today, I understood what is the most painful thing in the world.'

Falak glanced at her.

'To lose someone whom you never had.'

Falak went into a thoughtful trance while Nityami continued.

'It's painful because you had imagined a life with a person. Your entire love story with that person was in your mind. And because it was in your mind, your system had accepted it as something real. My love story with Vedant was one of these. Now I wish I hadn't come here to meet him. I wish I had continued keeping him in my mind till my last breath. I wish I had married whoever came first and not let my hope of meeting Vedant someday stay alive in me.'

Falak understood the tears Nityami was shedding. She had done that long ago. Acceptance blurs a lot of things which ego doesn't, she had realized, and therein lay its therapeutic nature. Truth be told, Falak had kept it alive first as a good memory and then, with time, it had taken on the status of a dream. As if Vedant had never happened to her. As if it was all wishful thinking, a fantasy for her stemming from the brutal reality she lived on a daily basis.

The girls sat in silence watching the even quieter lake. It must have given company to the happiness and sadness of so many people. It made them quiet from within. An hour later, they stood up and without saying anything to each other, walked to their cab. It drove them back to the homestay. As Tshering saw them getting down from the car, he came up to them with Romeo following.

'Vedant sir came back. Did you guys meet him at the lake?' he asked.

'We did,' Falak said, realizing Nityami wouldn't talk so easily.

The sadness in her voice caught Tshering's attention.

'I have a feeling you already know.'

'We do. He is here with his girlfriend Nitya,' Falak responded.

Tshering shook his head in disagreement.

'This is the reason why I said he isn't just a guest. He is a responsibility. Vedant sir stays here alone. Not with his girlfriend.'

Just when the girls thought they were done with life's jokes, life tickled them again.

*

8

What Tshering told them about Vedant zapped the girls. They returned to their room quietly. Before entering, they glanced at the door of Vedant's room but neither had the courage to knock. It wasn't some adventure that had made him stay in Lachen for so many months. According to Tshering, the first time Vedant had come here was with Nitya almost ten months ago. They stayed in the bigger room together. They both seemed like the perfect couple who were supposed to get married a year later. Or so they told Tshering when they were checking in. They were to stay for three nights before returning home. They had already travelled most of Sikkim before coming here.

It was on the second morning that Nitya was nowhere to be found. Tshering, Romeo and an anxious Vedant looked for her everywhere until their car was found in an abyss en route to the lake. The authorities were called and Nitya's body was pulled up, which was dangling from a tree below. She was dead. Because there was no eyewitness to the incident, it was presumed that Nitya had driven out from Tshering's homestay in the morning and her car must have skidded as there were marks on the road where the car had toppled and dropped down below.

When Nitya's body was pulled up and Vedant had been called to identify it, he fainted the moment he saw her. And remained unconscious for two days. His parents were called from Mumbai. When he woke up, he behaved as if Nitya was still alive. Tshering didn't remember what the medical condition exactly was, but he recalled what the doctor who had been flown in by his parents explained to them. Vedant had faced a trauma and his mind was unable to accept it. Thus his brain was stuck in a time loop of that very morning. Every day he woke up and sometimes didn't sleep so he could save Nitya. His mind had sold the idea to him that if he was awake, he wouldn't have allowed Nitya to drive and the catastrophe wouldn't have happened. From the next day onwards, he started driving off to the lake multiple times during the day. It was his emotional attempt to overcome the happenings of that day. In his conscious mind, Nitya was still alive. Though the rest of his memory was still intact. Tshering told them that his parents tried to take Vedant away from Lachen but he turned so violent that he almost hit them. They eventually appointed Tshering as Vedant's man Friday here, giving him a monthly salary.

'What was the solution?' the girls asked.

'The doctor had given him some medicines but he said Vedant would recover on his own when his mind accepted that Nitya was dead. And then he may be emotionally broken but at least he wouldn't be a prisoner of that particular moment in time when Nitya died. Until that day comes, Vedant continues to stay here.'

Acceptance, the ultimate emotional medicine, Falak thought.

Destiny had thrown a weird twist in the tale for Nityami. He'd recognized her but she wouldn't be able to profess her love to him. Not in this current state. And nobody knew when he would be emotionally all right. What should she do? Wait? For what? She had her job in Bhopal. She would probably get married to Hemant now that she knew the truth about Vedant. Maybe she would have had kids by the time Vedant got his emotional shit right.

As the girls came back to their room, they were quiet. Nityami lay down thinking. She noticed Falak too lying down on the other side of the bed. Then suddenly woke up in the wee hours of dawn to see Falak already sitting up on the bed.

'Damn, you scared me,' Nityami said. Falak only glanced at her with a stoic face.

'I have to leave,' Nityami said. Their eye-lock told the other both were contemplating the same thing.

'My purpose of coming here was different. Yours was more specific. It was to seek out Vedant. I was happy to find Vedant here but I can't see him like this, so I think I'll accompany you till Gangtok and then figure out where I should go,' Falak said so softly that Nityami didn't understand whether she was talking to herself or to her.

'Okay,' Nityami said. Both lay down on the bed again but neither slept. A few hours later, in the morning, Nityami got up first. She went to the window, which was welcoming the sun's rays inside. She saw Vedant downstairs having noodles. The sight pained her, for now, she knew his story. Yet, before leaving for Gangtok later in the day, she thought of approaching him for a one-to-one talk. She took a shawl and wrapped it around her body. She moved out of the room. This time not stopping by the mirror.

'Hey, Vedant,' she said, joining him.

'Nityami, how are you doing? You're putting up here?'

'Yeah, I am.'

'Another coincidence. For how many days?'

'Leaving today.'

'What? This place deserves to be stayed back in. Like Nitya is crazy about the place. This is the third time we have come here.'

'That's true. But I have work in Bhopal. And only so much leave.' Nityami felt choked talking so formally to Vedant. In her mind, in these years, she had indulged in so many imaginary yet intimate encounters that this seemed like the dullest version of their rendezvous that there could be.

'By the way,' Vedant said, 'we are getting married next year. Do give me your number. I'll invite you. It's always good to meet old friends.'

Nityami turned away to wipe her moist eyes and then looking at Vedant said, 'You give me your number. I'll WhatsApp.' She wouldn't, she knew.

'Sure.' Vedant gave his phone number, which Nityami pretended to save in her phone. *What irony*, she thought at the moment. She was dying to get his number and now when he was mouthing it himself, she wasn't even punching it in her phone.

'I just wanted to tell you . . .' Nityami tried her best but those words—*that I always loved you, will always do*—didn't come up through her choked voice.

'Yeah, tell me.'

'That I always liked you as a person.' Nityami had to change 'love' to 'liked'. And between the change, she knew she had grown up within.

'Thank you so much. You were always an amazing friend. I remember how you helped me with Hindi during school. I sucked at it. Forever indebted.'

Nityami knew if she stood there one more second, she'd cry her heart out.

Vedant looked at his watch and said, 'You have to excuse me. I need to drive Nitya to the lake.'

Vedant hugged her and whispered in her ear, 'Hope to see you soon.' He left. Nityami turned and started walking briskly. The walk soon turned into a run to . . . nowhere. When she stopped at a lonely place some distance from the homestay, she stood looking at the snow-capped mountains in the distance. She cried out loud like a baby who was shown a toy and then had it snatched right from her hand.

Two hours later, Nityami watched as the driver loaded her luggage in the car's boot. She had asked Tshering, who had arranged for a cab till Gangtok. She was about to sit in when she saw Falak standing thoughtfully at the side.

'What happened?' Nityami asked.

'I won't leave. I want to stay here with Vedant,' Falak said, averting her eyes from Nityami.

*

9

Nityami didn't ask Falak why she intended to stay back. She gave her a hug.

'Stay in touch,' she whispered in her ear and got inside the cab. As it took her back on to the zigzag road bordered by beatific nature, Nityami got deeply introspective. Where was she heading? Her home. To her parents. To Hemant. To her job. Was she happy there? If she was, she wouldn't have lied to them and come here seeking Vedant. If she was content with whatever she had in life, she wouldn't have kept Vedant alive in her. Then she asked herself again: *Where was she heading?* Nityami reclined her head on the seat back, turned a little towards the window and kept thinking.

She called Hemant.

'Hey, how are you?' Hemant asked. He always sounded so positive hearing her voice that she knew he would never disappoint her in life. But would she be able to do the same with him? Did she really love him or did she enjoy the fact that he listened to her? The two were different things. And, after meeting Vedant, it was all the more clear. Her love would just be one. Vedant. The rest would be her best bet to settle down into society's expectations.

'What if I never come back to you?' she asked.

The question was so direct that Hemant had no other option but to answer it straight. But he chose to ask a question in turn to clarify it for himself.

'As in there's a third person, is it? Vedant?'

'No. There's no third person. Not even Vedant. Now answer the question.'

Hemant had never heard such a serious Nityami before.

'I'll be sad and then I'll move on perhaps. That's the normal thing to do, I believe.' After a pause, he added, 'I hope you didn't mind that.'

'No. But would you easily move on? Like how easily one moves on from a person also shows a lot about his or her attachment to the person, right?'

'Of course, it does.'

There was silence. Nityami didn't say anything because she felt Hemant was figuring out something important to say. And he did.

'Do you know the difference between emotional healing and emotional cure?'

'I'm listening.'

'I never told you this but you have been an emotional cure for me. And thus, I won't be able to move on easily. Everyone wants to be close to their cure. Who knows when one needs it in life? While emotional healing is a personal process. The process may be triggered by someone but it would be accomplished only by the self.'

'Acceptance is the catalyst in that, right?'

'Right. You have been my cure, Nityami. I never said it. But every night when we sat having ice creams, I went home a slightly changed man. And the more I changed, the more I wanted you beside me. In the beginning, I wanted you only as my wife. But by then with time, I figured, the form of the relationship doesn't matter with your cure. You could be my friend or wife or whatever, but the important thing for me was that you were around.'

Tears escaped Nityami's eyes. Hemant had given words to what she had felt for Vedant.

'While healing makes you ready for the world once again, and thus makes the moving on part easier once healed.'

'Like you won't require the person any more in your life if you're healed?'

'Precisely.'

Maybe Vedant had triggered a healing process within her and thus she was now okay to leave him. Nityami pondered.

'I'll call you later.' Nityami ended the call. If everyone's ultimate option is to move on, Nityami wondered, then what's the fuss about? Then why not try something that isn't normal? Which may not become your comfort zone but will stay with you as a magical experience even if you have to move on eventually? That's when she understood why perhaps Falak had stayed back. Maybe she had nothing to go back to. While what Nityami was going back to, Hemant, could be hers sometime later in life as well. And even if it wasn't, would she care much? She realized she was basically living that moment of her life when one had to be absolutely and brutally honest with oneself, for the life that was waiting would either be an echo of this honesty or of the pretence that she was anyway living all through.

Nityami looked at the GPS. She had travelled halfway from Lachen to Gangtok. But during this time, she had travelled a lot within herself to realize Gangtok or Bhopal wasn't her destination. Not just yet. She had lived enough of 'what if' situations in her mind regarding Vedant. She had suffered enough for others' faults. She had limited her life enough to fit into what others had conditioned her to think for herself.

'Take me back, please,' she told the driver. He gave her a look and said, 'Madam, it will cost you . . .'

'I don't mind paying,' she said aloud and thought, *I've already paid enough.*

Falak went to the spot from where Nitya had supposedly fallen and died. She had a different battle in her mind. Had Nitya not died, she wouldn't have met Vedant here. In fact, she wouldn't have met Nityami either. From what she understood, Nityami got to know from a common friend that Vedant was in Gangtok and she planned a trip here, thereby meeting her in the process. If Vedant was in Mumbai with his girlfriend, Nityami would have known it from their common friends and would have carried on with her life. While Falak would have come here, stayed back for seven or eight days and then gone back to Delhi to carry on with life. Why did Nitya die? No, she didn't ask the question as it's asked in a murder mystery. It was more of an existential query. One accidental death and three lives somewhere changed and were set in motion to meet.

Falak was trying to grasp a deeper meaning in all this. Especially the fact that she wasn't here on a vacation. She had to end the evils of her life for the journey. She had no regret about what she had done to her father or boyfriend. If she hadn't done what she had, they would have continued to disturb her and Razia's lives in ways only they knew about.

Falak was brought out of her self-introspection with a car's horn. She looked up at the road to see Vedant's car. He waved at her. She waved back and approached him.

'What are you doing here?' he asked.

'Just taking in the nature around.'

Vedant stopped the car's engine and got down to join Falak. He went a little ahead and then turned to come back to the car.

'Can we go someplace else, please?' he asked.

Falak understood the spot must have triggered something in him.

'Sure.'

Vedant drove her to a nearby café. It was actually someone's home with a view and a few seats. They were served steaming tea as they settled down. The café served nothing else. Nobody was around except for the man who served them.

'Seems like light years ago; our college life,' Vedant said.

'Actually!'

'How is your father doing? I remember you always told me how you rebelled at home,' Vedant said, sipping his tea, holding the cup with both hands. Falak remembered he used to do the same in college too.

'You remember? That's surprising. He is doing fine, thank you.'

Vedant sipped his tea and glanced at Falak as if he had something to tell her. She shrugged, feeling the vibe.

'I said this to Nitya as well.'

'What? About my father?'

'No!' Vedant was amused. 'That I knew how much you loved me.'

It was a verbal checkmate for Falak. She didn't know what her next words should be.

'But it was me who pretended with whatever bullshit reason I gave at that time.'

'Does it mean you too used to . . .'

'I don't know that. I think lots of us in hindsight interpret a little bit of emotional or physical inclination as love. I don't want to do that. Though I remember the card you'd given me.'

'We can skip that stupidity. I won't mind. You returned the card anyway,' Falak said with a slight smile.

Vedant smiled and added, 'I always knew you were a strong-minded girl. And I knew I wouldn't be able to handle someone like you. Not that I'm saying it is a flaw of yours. I thought it was my flaw. And I knew it would, over time, destroy what we would have built by then. From what I knew then, ego never enters a relationship at the beginning. It always does once the relationship settles a bit.'

There were two ways to look at what Vedant had said. Either he was a chauvinist or he was someone who knew his weaknesses. The way he confessed told Falak that Vedant was the latter. People talked less about such men.

'So, somewhere I never deserved you,' Vedant said in a conclusive tone. Only Falak knew how much ego-squashing was required on a man's part to tell a girl that he didn't deserve her because of his inner flaws. She fell once again in love with him, then and there, if such a thing was possible.

'I had to tell you this.' He had finished his tea by then. Falak hadn't sipped hers even once. She had been with a guy who used to unleash his ego on her body knowing well she was on a higher level than him in every which way possible. And here was a guy who hadn't even touched her, knowing the very same fact. In the moment, Falak felt proud to be in love with Vedant even though she knew there was no fruition to this. It was a lost cause. But sometimes, she understood, lost causes were better than requited ones.

'Oh, let's go now,' he said, looking at his watch. Falak didn't ask why.

They soon reached Tshering's homestay. As Vedant parked his SUV, Falak saw Nityami and a smile escaped her. She went to her and gave her a tight hug.

'I hoped you would be back,' Falak said.

'Thanks for making me a part of your hope. Nobody ever did that before,' Nityami said and hugged her back tighter. Somewhere their pain was similar, even though the source, the expression and the consumption of it by both of them were different.

*

10

The next week went by with them accompanying Vedant to Gurudongmar Lake. The girls had divided the days. Monday-Wednesday-Friday, Nityami was supposed to tag along with Vedant to the lake. While on Tuesdays, Thursdays and Saturdays, it was Falak. On Sunday, the girls used to go with Vedant together. And it was their first Sunday together. Neither realized how the seven days went by.

When Falak called Razia on Monday and told her about Vedant's story, she understood perhaps Falak wasn't coming back.

'Don't worry. Your clients have taken a liking to me. Now, you don't be jealous!'

'Jealous? I'm the happiest, Razia sweety.'

'Have you decided what you are going to do there? And for how long?'

'Both Nityami and I've decided that we would go with the flow for some time.'

'But what about the expenses?'

'I'll figure something out, Razia sweety.'

'Let me transfer 25 per cent of the income I'm getting here. Anyway, it is your business.'

'A business belongs to the one who runs it. So, you do what you're doing. If possible, just transfer 10 per cent to me.'

'Done.'

On Tuesday, when Nityami was staying put at the homestay, she had a call with her parents.

'I'll be home soon, papa. But I'll have to come back here again immediately.'

'Why?'

'I'm taking a transfer to Kolkata for some time,' Nityami lied through her teeth.

'Transfer?' It was her mother. 'But why?'

'That's because the bank I work for isn't owned by Papa. Come on, mummy, transfer is the normal thing in government jobs.'

'I'll explain it to her, beta,' her father said.

It was the following Sunday when the two sat together. Nityami felt happy right from her core having noodles sitting with Falak.

'Can I confess something?'

'Sure.'

'This is the happiest moment of my life.' Nityami had a pure smile on her face as she said it.

'Having Maggi noodles?'

'No! I never had the kind of clarity in my heart like I have right now.'

Falak reached out and pinched her hard. 'Same to you.'

'I know we agreed that we would not ask each other about Vedant but I'm so curious if you guys had some conversation. He remains quiet with me.'

'You remain quiet with him. I've realized Vedant is more responsive than the one who initiates things.'

'True that. But I don't know why, I love being silent with him.'

Falak smiled.

'I want to confess something,' Falak said. What Nityami heard in the next half hour was a verbal biopic of Falak. And it ended with exactly why she was here in Lachen. Nityami couldn't believe it. She thought she was the one with whom life was being unfair, but hearing Falak's story, Nityami realized she was actually blessed to have what she did.

'Did you really get pregnant?' Nityami asked and Falak nodded. Nityami felt the knots in her stomach just thinking of being in Falak's place. Any other girl would have been tamed. Not Falak Sultana. It told Nityami about the kind of spirit Falak had. If the latter had confessed her dark experiences to anyone else, he or she would have judged her, perhaps thought of her as a murderer, but Nityami chose to focus on the inspirational side of Falak. She understood exactly why she had to take that drastic step. It was similar to what she had done to Raghav and his fiancée. She didn't kill someone but she did kill the relationship. The intention, for Nityami, justified the outcome.

Neither girl spoke much for quite some time. Then Falak suddenly spoke up, 'Let's go out.'

'Sure, but I need to tell you something as well.'

'Don't tell me you too have a killer inside you.'

'I do, but of a different kind,' Nityami said and passed Falak her phone, opening a particular app. Falak took the phone with a confused glance. One look and she couldn't believe what she saw.

'You hacked this bitch's profile?' Falak asked, seeing Naagin Ki Naani's page.

'It's me.'

For a moment, Falak couldn't speak. Then she didn't get the right words. In the end, she burst out laughing at the irony that they both were.

In the evening, the two set up a bonfire, collecting wood from the vicinity and sat down beside it.

'What's the plan? All I know is we are here as long as Vedant is here.' Nityami began the conversation.

'Which is forever,' Falak said.

'But there's hope of him moving out of the loop.'

'Well, I know, but nobody knows when that will happen. Till then, what do we do? I will lose my MBA.'

'Before I forget, I would love to talk to Razia. She is so kick-ass. I wish I had such a stepmother.'

'Talk to your dad.'

Both laughed. Then Nityami said, 'I'll lose Hemant. My job. And parents . . . umm, I think they will eventually accept me.'

'But the question is, what do we do here before our savings get over?'

'Let's put together what we feel on paper and then match our notes. Let's see if our plans overlap or not. If they do, we will have our answer.'

'If they don't?'

'They will. If we fell for the same guy, we will fall for the same plan as well,' Nityami said. Falak gave her a high five.

They heard a car's engine starting. Both rushed out to see Vedant starting his SUV.

'Vedant!'

The next moment, the girls approached him.

'Can we join you?' Nityami asked.

'We won't come between Nitya and you. Promise!' Falak quipped jocularly. Vedant looked at them and said, 'Hop in, girls!'

They sat in Vedant's SUV and headed towards Gurudongmar Lake. As they parked the car and went to sit by the lake, they noticed there were a few visitors that day. Vedant chose the particular spot where they found him on the first day.

The three sat in silence looking over the grand lake. In their hearts, the girls knew what they had decided would put them in the middle of uncertainties. But they also knew at the heart of those uncertainties lay their true potential as individuals.

Falak leaned towards Nityami and said in a hush-hush tone, 'Can we collaborate on the Naagin Ki Naani profile?

'I just deleted it.'

'What the hell, why?'

Nityami thought for some time and whispered back, 'Because Naagin Ki Naani 2.0 is supposed to come up.' She winked at Falak.

'Girls, please. Nitya likes it quiet.'

The two girls put their fingers on their lips immediately.

*

11

Tshering approached the girls when they were out in the morning for a walk. It was their sixteenth day at the homestay. He was accompanied by Romeo.

'Hey Tshering, how's it going?' Falak asked.

'Going good, madam. I wanted to ask you something.'

'About our lunch?' Nityami asked. It was only over food that they used to talk to Tshering.

'No, madam. I was actually getting some stay requests from other guests. But I don't know how long you two will be here so I'm not able to take up those requests.'

Falak and Nityami glanced at each other. They were so engrossed in their own life, that they forgot they hadn't told Tshering about their exit plans.

'May we please tell you about it tonight?' Falak asked.

'Sure, sure, madam. No hurry. I just wanted to know, that's all.'

Tshering and Romeo went away.

'So, what's our exit plan?' Nityami turned to Falak.

'None. But we need a staying plan.'

That evening, Falak and Nityami started brainstorming about ways they could stay back in Lachen. And they knew it couldn't be just about their staying.

'I can't be on leave forever,' Nityami said.

'And I can't live forever on my savings,' Falak lamented.

'We need a plan which would answer questions about our sustenance and staying here together.'

A good one hour of debating later, Falak wondered why she couldn't do here what she was doing in Delhi.

'I can replicate my tiffin service here.'

'But there aren't as many people. A tiffin service works for people in the city where they are too busy to give time to the kitchen.'

Nityami had a point.

Falak paced up to the window. She casually looked out. She could see Tshering's homestay board outside. Then she noticed Tshering bringing in two bags full of groceries. And walking towards his house.

Falak turned with sudden excitement.

'I have an idea!'

The very next day, Nityami took a cab and after being driven for seven-odd hours reached Bagdogra Airport. She flew to Bhopal unannounced. The excitement of the plan the two girls hatched had to be immediately acted upon.

Her parents were surprised to see her. And then they were worried hearing her plans.

'How can you start a business in . . . which place is this? Is this even in India?' Her mother asked.

'Lachen. Very much in India, mummy. And how means what? I have a business partner. Falak.'

There was a cross-examination for an hour between mother and daughter. The father was quiet all through. He was only studying his daughter. And then suddenly spoke up after an hour.

'Both your mummy and I are sorry, Nityami,' he said. Nityami gave him a puzzled look. So did her mother.

'We took a long time to realize you are a grown-up now. And you have the right to do whatever you want.'

Nityami's mother's jaw dropped.

'I'm with your decision, beta. Just take care of yourself. You know how I hate it when you're upset. Just be happy always.'

Nityami almost leapt on to her father, hugging him tight and crying her heart out.

'I promise I'll be safe and in touch always. After I settle the business a little, you two also shift there.'

In the evening, she met Hemant and told him her plans. Of business and also the truth.

'I don't love you, Hemant, and you deserve to settle down with someone who loves you. Everyone does.'

Hemant looked at her and smiled. 'I knew that. But I knew I would never get someone like you, so I willingly wanted to be okay with the idea of settling with someone I was in love with.'

'I'm sorry, Hemant.'

'Don't be. I totally get it. For you, cutting the cords of conditioning was important.'

There, Nityami thought, that's what she was doing. Cutting the cords of social conditioning and trying to live exactly the way her heart wanted to. Not trapped by the past, not worried about the future. Just in love, in being, in sync with the present.

It was their last ice cream together. Once they finished, Hemant dropped her home. No words were spoken.

The next day, Nityami went to her bank and put in her papers. Two days later, she was back in Lachen. This time with a lot more luggage. And renewed hope.

When Nityami entered the homestay room, she noticed Falak working on one of the walls. She had scribbled all over the wall. Registering Nityami's presence, Falak turned to her.

'Don't worry about the wall. Tshering won't mind this.'

Nityami relaxed. She knew her face was radiating the anxiety she felt inside thinking if she had to pay for the painting of the wall.

'I've talked with Tshering. He is in. This is the detailed business plan. Study it and let me know what you think.'

Nityami looked at the whiteboard. And the first word that caught her attention was the one written in caps.

FNT's Soul Food 'N' Stay.

And it was obvious what FNT stood for. Falak-Nityami-Tshering.

ELEVEN MONTHS LATER

The house which used to be Tshering's homestay now read: FNT's SOUL FOOD 'N' STAY.

Falak and Nityami chalked out a business plan using Falak's five-semester MBA knowledge. She had forgone the sixth and final semester and so, couldn't secure her MBA. But the knowledge was enough for her to design a plan to offer people food and stay. Not just noodles like before. Falak took care of the food, Nityami took care of the finances where her experience as a banker proved useful, while Tshering looked after the administration and the housekeeping part. Nityami also did the online marketing for the place. Her luck as Naagin Ki Naani rubbed off on this as well and ended up drawing quite a good number of followers with 100 per cent positive reviews.

That was not all. Vedant, seeing the girls get on with the daily business, started sitting at the front and played the role of cashier to perfection without even being offered the job. They were more than happy to accommodate him in their business. His only breaks were the time he drove out along with 'Nitya' to the lake. But once he was back, he took on his role again. It was a dream run for both the girls. For it wasn't just a business they were running. It stood for their control over their lives. Their rebellion against what life had shaped them up to be before this.

One morning, it started with the usual humdrum routine. Since Lachen was one sure-shot location before Gurudongmar Lake, it had become the go-to place for a lot of tourists, cab drivers and some locals as well. The routine started at six in the morning and remained so till 7 p.m.

Falak was usually busy in the kitchen. They had three workers under her. Nityami was finishing her morning call with her parents. She was arranging their visit to Lachen. Calls with Hemant had stopped. Two months before the present day, Hemant had WhatsApp-ed her his wedding card.

This is more of information than invite, he had written.

All the best, she had replied.

In the next two minutes, she couldn't see Hemant's DP on her WhatsApp. She understood the obvious.

Once the call with her parents was over, she logged into FNT's social media pages and was busy boosting the posts for greater reach while checking the recent Google reviews, when Tshering came running to her.

'Falak madam . . .' he said. Nityami sensed something was wrong. She followed Tshering out. She saw Falak moving out of the premises with a lady and two men who looked like cops but were in civil dress. Nityami hurried to her.

'Hey, what happened?'

Falak turned. Her solemn face told Nityami her worst nightmares had come true.

'I knew this would happen one day, Nityami,' Falak said.

'What? Who are these people?'

'Delhi Police. I'm being arrested for the murder of Abbu and Wasim.' There was no remorse in her voice. Just self-pity.

'How am I supposed to run FNT without you?' Nityami started, but Falak interjected.

'Come what may, you'll continue FNT, Nityami. Promise me. If proven guilty, I may get a life term but I'll be back. I already have a flow chart in mind. Just don't give up on me. I'll ask Razia to get in touch with you.'

Falak hugged Nityami. The latter realized Falak's body was mildly shivering.

'I'll be here. Waiting for you to come,' Nityami whispered in her ear.

'Take care. Of yourself. And Vedant,' Falak whispered back.

As they broke their embrace, there was prolonged eye contact. They fed assurances to the other. After which the lady officer pulled Falak away. They made her get into the Innova they had come in and then drove off. Nityami, with Tshering and Romeo behind her, kept looking at the disappearing car with crestfallen faces.

'Where's Vedant?' Nityami asked.

'I saw him walking out half an hour before these people came looking for Falak madam.'

Nityami moved out of the FNT premises and headed towards the main road. With every step, she felt her heart getting heavier. Only she knew how much she was fighting to keep her tears at bay.

A little on to the road, she saw Vedant at a distance. He was standing at the same spot where Nitya had supposedly fallen off the edge in her car. As Nityami went closer, she could hear his muffled sobs.

'Vedant, what happened?' Nityami asked. She was still in two minds whether she should tell him about Falak's arrest. But his sobs made her guess he probably knew already. Did he see her being taken away?

Nityami tapped his shoulder. He turned. His eyes were bloodshot.

'Nitya is no more!' He held Nityami tight and cried on. And Nityami wondered if Vedant had finally accepted the ugly truth of his life.

She held him by his hands, took him inside the FNT premises and asked Tshering to get in touch with his parents immediately.

What if Vedant became normal now? What if he goes back to Mumbai to his original life? What if Falak actually gets life imprisonment? What if she had to run FNT only with Tshering? What if . . .

Life had once again thrown her in the middle of a lot of 'what-ifs'. But this Nityami was different. She wouldn't swim in confusion. She knew where she was at that moment in time. The present. And that was enough.

Nityami turned and raised her confident voice so Tshering could hear her loud and clear.

'We need to urgently employ a chef, Tshering. Let's get going.'

* * *

Acknowledgements

Heartfelt thanks and gratitude to:

Milee Ashwarya—Can't thank you enough for being the constant source of motivation.

Ralph—for the smooth edits. Was a pleasure working on yet another book with you.

The entire team at Penguin Random House India, for their constant support.

Friends and family—for being there whenever I need you all.

R—for protecting my innocence.

Scan QR code to access the
Penguin Random House India website